Love Unfeigned
A Pride and Prejudice Variaton
MJ Stratton

Love Unfeigned
A Pride and Prejudice Variation
Copyright 2025 by MJ Stratton
Cover design by Pemberley Darcy
All rights reserved.

Amazon Edition
ISBN: 9798309331406

This book is a work of fiction. Any person or place appearing herein is fictitious or is used fictitiously.

All rights reserved, including the right to reproduce this book, or portions thereof, in any form. No portion of this book may be reproduced in any form without written permission from the publisher or author, except as permitted by U.S. copyright law.

NO AI TRAINING: Without in any way limiting the author's exclusive rights under copyright, any use of this publication to "train" generative artificial intelligence (AI) technologies to generate text is expressly **prohibited**. The author reserves all rights to license uses of this work for generative AI training and development of machine learning language models.

This eBook is licensed for personal use only and may not be re-sold or given away to others. If you would like to share this book with another person, please purchase an additional copy

LOVE UNFEIGNED

for each person. If you're reading this book and did not purchase it, or it was not purchased for your use only, then please purchase your copy.

Thank you for respecting the hard work of this author.

Contents

Dedication	VII
About the Book	1
1. Chapter 1	3
2. Chapter 2	7
3. Chapter 3	11
4. Chapter 4	16
5. Chapter 5	21
6. Chapter 6	26
7. Chapter 7	31
8. Chapter 8	36
9. Chapter 9	42
10. Chapter 10	48
11. Chapter 11	53
12. Chapter 12	57
13. Chapter 13	61
14. Chapter 14	66
15. Chapter 15	71
16. Chapter 16	75

17.	Chapter 17	79
18.	Chapter 18	84
19.	Chapter 19	88
20.	Chapter 20	92
21.	Chapter 21	96
22.	Chapter 22	100
23.	Chapter 23	107
24.	Chapter 24	111
	Epilogue	115
	Other Books by MJ Stratton	120
	Acknowledgements	122
	About The Author	123

Dedication

For Rebecca McBrayer
Thanks for cheering me on, and for your kind words about the story!

About the Book

Escape to London? Elizabeth Bennet is happy to. Her mother has been unbearable ever since Elizabeth refused to marry her odious cousin. Besides which, her beloved sister Jane is in London, heartbroken, and much in need of Elizabeth's help. Jane's recovery from her suitor's defection is utmost in Elizabeth's mind, until she receives a letter filled with romantic sentiments from the only source less likely than her already-refused cousin, the aggravating, arrogant, obnoxious Mr. Darcy.

Darcy has tried to purge Elizabeth Bennet from his thoughts and heart, but her fine eyes and pert opinions haunt him even in his sleep. When a letter arrives from Elizabeth Bennet, the machinations of someone close to him come to light. Delighted at the chance to pursue inclination rather than expectation, Darcy continues the correspondence started by another.

When untold truths surface, Elizabeth must decide if she can trust the gentleman with whom she has fallen deeply in love, and Darcy must do everything he can to persuade her that he is not the same unfeeling man she despised in Hertfordshire. Love Unfeigned is a sweet, low-angst Darcy and Elizabeth novella that brings an early happily ever after for our dear couple.

January 1812
Darcy House
Georgiana

Georgiana Darcy watched her brother, concern filling her heart. He had not been himself since he returned to London at the end of last November. His reserved nature, usually absent when in the privacy of their home, seemed ever present. He gazed at nothing as though deep in thought, and his lips often turned down into a decidedly unhappy expression.

If I did not know any better, I would think someone had died. Georgiana wondered if her brother's preoccupation had something to do with her folly. Last summer, she had most unwisely attempted to elope with the son of their father's former steward. It had not come to fruition—her brother had come to the house in Ramsgate unexpectedly, and she had felt compelled to tell him everything.

Never had she disappointed him more, and her shame had compounded until he departed for Hertfordshire last autumn. His letters had been full of the usual tidbits about the neighborhood, and he had mentioned a few of the families more than once.

A strange idea crept into Georgiana's mind, and she almost dismissed it out of hand. *No,* she thought. *It is not possible. My brother? In love?* The idea seemed tantalizingly close to the truth. Glancing across the room, she observed her usually unflappable brother. He sat forward with his elbows on his knees and his hands clasped beneath his chin. Fitzwilliam stared into the fire, and she thought she detected a look of pain in his expression.

If there was one thing Georgiana could recognize, it was a broken heart. *What happened in Hertfordshire?* she wondered. Like any good sister, she felt it was her duty to decipher her brother's strange mood. And so, on the following day, whilst Fitzwilliam was out, Georgiana crept into his rooms to have a look around.

The master's chambers had changed very little since her father died. They had changed the rug—it was now green, blue, and tan instead of red and gold. Heavy drapes matched the rug, and the furniture had been reupholstered as well. Fitzwilliam's rooms were in pristine condition—not a thing was out of place. His valet, Brisby, disliked clutter of any kind.

Georgiana drifted to the writing desk, hoping to find an explanation amongst her brother's letters. Carefully, she opened the writing case and leafed through the stack of letters inside. There were a few from Pemberley's steward and one from Lady Catherine that had yet to be opened. She recognized Mr. Bingley's untidy scrawl across one, and she picked it up. Unfolding the papers, she scanned the brief note.

Darcy,

I cannot help but think you are wrong. Miss Bennet surely loved me as I love her. I fear if I do not return to Hertfordshire, my heart will burst. Pray, come with me to Gentleman Jack's tomorrow—you can beat some sense into me.

Bingley

The note was dated the day previous—Fitzwilliam had gone to Gentleman Jack's that afternoon. Georgiana frowned. She recognized the name Bennet. Her brother had written of the family, but she did not recall the details. *I shall have to investigate my letters when I am finished here*, she thought. Moving Mr. Bingley's letter aside, she continued to leaf through her brother's letters. There was nothing in his correspondence to indicate why he might be suffering from depressed spirits.

Her gaze drifted to a stack of unfinished missives stacked neatly on one side of the writing box. There was one to the steward and another to Richard—Colonel Fitzwilliam. Huffing in irritation, Georgiana moved to stack the papers again. A single sheet slid out from the bottom of the stack and drifted silently to the floor. Curiously, she set the stack aside and retrieved the missive and read it.

Dearest, loveliest Elizabeth,

It has been two months since I beheld your face. Never have I known such agony! Your fine eyes haunt me in my sleep, twinkling with mischief in my dreams. How I long to caress your chocolate curls, to feel their silken texture wrapped around my fingers.

Performing my duty has never been the onerous and unwanted task it now seems. I have learned, from infancy, to take pride in my name and position. Being born to privilege comes with specific obligations, or so my mother and father taught me. Now, after so many years, I have cause to resent it all. Had I been born the son of a tradesman, or that of a minor country gentleman, I could have you. But your position in life, so decidedly beneath my own, prevents me from making you my wife.

Many nights I have attempted to convince myself that you and I are equals—I am a gentleman, and you are a gentleman's daughter. But alas, this is not enough to outweigh the drawbacks of offering for you. Your mother and younger sisters behave with an extreme lack of decorum. I know you understand, for I witnessed your mortification at the Netherfield Ball. Even your father could not exert himself to behave with propriety, I am sorry to say.

More than this, your connections to trade are impossible to overcome. What would my parents say if they knew I meant to offer the position of Mistress of Pemberley to one whose blood is so tainted?

If I raised your expectations, I am very sorry. When it came time for me to leave Hertfordshire, I thought it best to depart without bidding you farewell. I could not bear the grief in your eyes as you comprehended the truth of the situation. Dearest Elizabeth, please forgive me. Please understand that if I were a lesser man, I would give myself to you in but a moment. Our respective stations, vastly different, keep us apart.

I love you,

Fitzwilliam Darcy

Never had Georgiana read something so insulting and romantic at the same time. So, her brother was in love with Miss Elizabeth Bennet. She recalled the name—he had written of her many times, admiring her ability to put Miss Bingley in her place without slinging insults.

What is this drivel about position? she asked. Her brother's explanation about how marrying Mr. Wickham would lower *her* status rang in her mind. It was not the same in this situation. Marrying Elizabeth would raise the lady's status to that of his own. The connections to trade could not be so easily explained away, but she thought her brother rather hypocritical. His closest friend, besides Richard, was Mr. Bingley, a man whose fortune came from his father's success in trade. Miss Elizabeth held a greater position in society than Miss Bingley!

She would need time to think and plan. Fitzwilliam deserved happiness, and Georgiana would ensure he had it. It was the least she could do after her behavior last summer.

January 1812
Longbourn
Elizabeth

"The carriage will take you to Gracechurch Street tomorrow," Papa said wearily. "Your mother will not be content until you have left the house."

Elizabeth patted her father's hand soothingly. "I shall be happy to join Jane," she said. "There is nothing for it, you know. Mama ought to have known I would not be pressured into accepting Mr. Collins."

"Go pack your trunk." He waved her away. "Then come and see me. I shall send you with enough funds to enjoy yourself."

Elizabeth hurried out of the study and upstairs. She looked forward to her time away from Longbourn. Mrs. Bennet had been particularly shrill since Elizabeth had refused her father's cousin's offer of marriage. Mr. Collins was a sycophantic man with little sense. She did not care if he would inherit upon her father's death—she would not be trapped in a marriage with a fool.

"A letter for you, Miss Lizzy." Hill handed her a folded missive.

The paper felt thick and seemed to be of good quality. Turning it over, she felt a little jolt as she noted the direction. *Darcy House?* she thought in bemusement. "Thank you, Hill." Elizabeth climbed the stairs quickly, cognizant of Hill's stares boring into her back. Once safely in her chambers, she closed and locked the door before breaking the seal on the letter.

Dear Miss Elizabeth,

How the hours apart from you have wracked and tormented me. Never have I loved another as I love you, and I cannot bear to be parted from you any longer. It has now been more than two months since I last beheld your beloved face, and never in all my days have I known such agony. The very thought of your absence fills my heart with a sorrow that seems to grow deeper with every passing moment.

Your fine eyes, those enchanting orbs, haunt me even in my sleep, twinkling with mischief amidst my most vivid dreams. I find myself entranced by the thought of them, and yet I am lost without them before me. How often I long to caress your chocolate curls, to feel their silken texture wound about my fingers, and to bury my face in the sweetness of your presence.

I fear that my own deficiencies, my imperfections, may prove insurmountable, keeping me from your heart forever. But I beseech you, dearest, do not let that be so. For I would gladly endure any hardship, any humiliation, if it meant winning your favor and affections. My soul is bound to you, and I can no longer bear this distance. My heart calls for you with a strength that neither time nor space can diminish.

I remain, in all things, yours most devotedly,
Fitzwilliam Darcy

Elizabeth felt hot and cold all at once. *Mr. Darcy loves me?* she thought incredulously. She hardly knew what to do or what to think. He breached all bounds of propriety by sending her this missive. They were not attached, and a small part of her resented him for presuming so much. If anyone discovered the letter, she would be forced to marry him! And that could not be so. He was insufferable at best.

You do not truly think that, a wicked little voice whispered in her mind. *You were offended, your vanity wounded by his intemperate words at the assembly.* It was true, and she knew it in her heart. But there was more to the situation. Mr. Darcy had demonstrated his contempt for Elizabeth and all her neighbors in every word and deed. He kept himself aloof and made no effort to be friendly. *And it is very likely his fault that Jane is left heartbroken.*

A thread of an idea crept into her thoughts. *If* Mr. Darcy had helped to separate Jane and Mr. Bingley, then could Elizabeth use his affection for *her* to enable her dearest sister to know happiness? The idea had merit. Mr. Bingley and Mr. Darcy were very good friends. If Elizabeth were engaged to Mr. Darcy, she could ensure her most deserving sister could have her happiness.

But am I to sacrifice my life for another's? She did not love Mr. Darcy—she had not loved Mr. Collins either. She and Jane had resolved to marry only for the deepest of affection, and the only feelings she could ascribe to the haughty gentleman from the north were dislike and vexation. Except... She read the letter again. Her heart thumped painfully in her chest. Already there was more between her and Mr. Darcy than Mr. Collins could ever boast.

Elizabeth thought back to the assembly. She had admired him immediately. His handsome features were obvious even across the assembly hall. When the party had been introduced to the Bennets, she had hoped he would ask for a dance. Her disappointment when he had not had been brushed off, though the hurt had compounded when he declared her *tolerable* and not *handsome enough* to tempt him.

This letter proved he thought a great deal more of her than what he had professed at their first meeting. *Should I take the chance?* she wondered. Elizabeth could not guarantee Hill would keep the missive private. If Mrs. Bennet were to find out Mr. Darcy had written to her, there would be no end to the harassment until Elizabeth became Mrs. Darcy.

I am for London anyway, she told herself. *If anything is to come from this, it is best to happen away from Mama's prying eyes.* Elizabeth sat on the edge of her bed for some time, carefully weighing the benefits against the drawbacks of replying to Mr. Darcy's letter. Positive outcomes outweighed the negative. Her good cheer would be a wonderful counter for his more somber manner.

But can you cure him of his disdain? She forced herself to ponder. Yes, she believed she could. Mama always said a man in love could be persuaded to do anything. *Mayhap I can even convince him to make amends with Mr. Wickham.* Decided, she put off packing her trunk and settled before her writing desk to pen a reply to the letter.

January 1812
London
Georgiana

The reply to Georgiana's forged letter came in mid-January. She had checked the post faithfully for days, hoping to intercept any reply before her brother saw it.

Hours she had spent, carefully practicing his script until hers looked similar enough to Fitzwilliam's to be ascribed to him. Georgiana had composed the first letter to Elizabeth in her own writing first before painstakingly copying it to fresh paper, her hand carefully forming the letters. The finished product, blot-free and acceptably romantic, was what seemed like the millionth iteration. The hand looked passably masculine, and enough like her brother's to be convincing.

Georgiana had gone to her letters to decipher Elizabeth's direction. The name of the estate, Longbourn, and the name Bennet had been enough. The nearby market town of Meryton had been the last detail she needed to add the direction to her missive. Now she would see if her efforts had paid off. Eagerly, she took the missive to her chambers, closing and locking the door before settling herself before the window.

Sunlight poured through the glass panes, warming her as she sat. The maid had tied her pink floral curtains back. Georgiana could see out onto the street. Carriages and carts passed by occasionally, but their noise did not reach her rooms.

Turning the missive over, she broke the seal. It was a very simple design; the calligraphic letter E had flowers surrounding it. The impression in the red wax spoke of the lady's appreciation of the outdoors. Fitzwilliam had described her propensity for walking in at least three letters. Breaking the seal, she unfolded the missive and read.

Dear Sir,

I confess to some consternation at your letter. Your feelings, so artfully expressed, were heartfelt and genuine. I must thank you for the honor of being the recipient of such tender affection. Honored though I am, I must express my complete shock at being thus addressed. When you and your party departed at the end of November, I had no inkling that you held any such regard for me. Indeed, I supposed you felt rather differently—perhaps even indifferently—towards me.

Surprised though I am, I cannot help but feel deeply touched by your words. They are sincere, and their eloquence strikes me more than I care to admit. They stand in stark contrast to those you uttered in October—'tolerable' and 'not handsome enough to tempt you.' Those words were like daggers to me and yet now I find myself torn between surprise and... something else.

How has your opinion changed so drastically, sir? How is it that the man who spoke with such clear disdain for me now writes in such earnest tones? I find myself wondering, with no small degree of bewilderment, if I misinterpreted your expressions in the past, if my own judgment was so faulty as to have misread your every glance and word. Your change in demeanor baffles me, though I find it impossible to not be curious—nay, even hopeful.

As you know, I pride myself on being an excellent judge of character, and this letter—so profoundly different from the man I once believed you to be—calls into question everything I have assumed about you. Where once there was pride and aloofness, there now exists an unexpected tenderness, a vulnerability I did not believe you capable of showing. How, sir, is this possible? I ask myself this question repeatedly as I struggle for the words to pen here. Already I have discarded three sheets of paper, my thoughts in disarray as I attempt to answer you with the sincerity your words deserve.

Are you perhaps more like my sister Jane than I had realized? She is so reserved, so cautious in revealing the depths of her heart, even to me, her most beloved sister. Her heartache these past months has been great enough that it cannot be concealed, though she would surely wish to hide it. And yet, your letter speaks of a similar pain, a sorrow so raw that I cannot help but feel a kinship between your words and the very emotions Jane has suffered. Is there a parallel between you and her, sir? A heart too proud, too guarded, to show its true feelings until they can no longer be hidden?

Pardon my candid nature, but I believe we have already moved past the point of mere social niceties. Direct speech, I trust, will serve us better now. Too many misunderstandings stand between us, and it would be a grave mistake to allow them to compound further.

If I have not been clear, sir, then I shall attempt to be so now. Your letter, despite the confusion it has caused me, has touched me deeply. My heart, which I believed firmly resolved against you, now finds itself entranced, and I can no longer deny the stirrings I feel. I would know more of you, sir, and learn if we may suit each other better than I ever thought possible.

Pray, do not concern yourself with thoughts that I would accept you for mercenary reasons. I have recently turned down a most eligible offer of marriage from my father's cousin and heir. Wealth and status hold no sway over me, for I would sooner remain free of a loveless marriage than to accept one for comfort or convenience. It is the heart's true desire—love unfeigned—that must guide us. If we are to wed, it will be because we find in each other a kindred spirit, one with whom we may share our lives, not merely for security or wealth.

Should our correspondence be discovered, rest assured that my father would insist on an honorable outcome, as he would with any of my sisters. But let us hope, at the very least, that we can speak freely, without fear of reproach, for there are many things I still wish to understand, to share with you.

I come to London on the morrow, and shall stay with my Aunt and Uncle Gardiner at Gracechurch Street. If you wish to be discreet, you may place your reply into the hands of the maid, Sally. She is illiterate and will not pry into your words.

With all sincerity,
Elizabeth Bennet

Georgiana folded the letter and sighed. "How romantic!" she said earnestly, speaking aloud in the empty room. "She is not indifferent to him; that much is clear. But what is this nonsense about being tolerable and not handsome enough?" What had her brother done? It seemed very unlike Fitzwilliam to insult a lady, especially upon the first meeting. The words about pride and disdain did not surprise Georgiana. Many thought such things about her brother. He kept himself above those with whom he had a slight acquaintance and nothing more. Too many matchmaking mamas had thrust their daughters in his direction. Even some of Georgiana's so-called friends had abandoned her when it became clear their quest to be Mrs. Darcy would be unsuccessful.

I must pen a reply directly, she thought. *Elizabeth is in London, too! Perhaps I can get them to meet. Oh, but it will take so long to copy the script so that it looks like my brother's.* Knowing she would be at it for hours, Georgiana settled into her chair and pulled a sheet of paper closer, determined to have another missive to send before the end of the day.

January, 1812
Gracechurch Street
Elizabeth

"Dear Jane!" Elizabeth embraced her sister before turning to her aunt and repeating the gesture. "How I missed you!"

"It has been but a few weeks," Jane replied, smiling thinly. She looked as though she had not been sleeping. Her eyes, usually happy, looked very sad. Jane's clothing hung a little looser, too, and Elizabeth wondered if her sister had been eating enough.

They went to the bedchamber they would share, and Elizabeth proceeded to empty her trunk. "Have you called upon the Bingley sisters?" she asked gently, hanging her sage green gown in the wardrobe.

"I did." Jane sat on the bed, tucking her feet beneath her. The cream gown she wore spread out around her, and she looked angelic. "I did so immediately upon my arrival. They returned the call this morning."

"Three weeks?" Elizabeth paused and turned an incredulous expression on her sister. "Their meaning is clear; surely, you see that!"

Jane shrugged indifferently. "They have many connections in town. Ours was slight enough that they likely do not have the time to entertain it."

"You do yourself a disservice," Elizabeth insisted. "Those two do not wish you to marry their brother and have cut the acquaintance, hoping to deter you." Frowning angrily, Elizabeth reached for another gown. "Do not give up, dearest." *Not now that I am corresponding with Mr. Darcy.* He would be Jane's savior—she felt it in her bones.

Jane stood. "I shall leave you to finish unpacking," she said listlessly. "I promised our cousins I would read them a story." Jane departed, leaving Elizabeth alone. The silence allowed her to think, and she contemplated her letter to Mr. Darcy. How carefully she had crafted it! The missive contained no untruths—she did not embellish sentiments she did not possess. Every word was honest. Now she would have to wait and see if her words offended the man and drove him off, or if she would receive another letter.

The afternoon passed quickly, and soon she joined her aunt, uncle, and sister at the table for the evening meal. The children had dined earlier and were in bed, leaving the adults to speak together without interruption.

"We are very pleased to have you here, Elizabeth," her uncle, Mr. Edward Gardiner, said as he cut his meat. "Your aunt has selected several bolts of fabric from my warehouse, ready for making into gowns."

"Thank you, Uncle. Papa sent enough funds for me and Jane. I hope we shall have several excursions to Bond Street whilst I am here." Elizabeth smiled and put a bite into her mouth.

"You will doubtless wish to go to Hatchard's," her aunt, Madeline Gardiner, quipped. "Do not spend all your pin money on books, I beg you!"

"Never!" Elizabeth laughed, noting absently that her humor had not even prompted a small smile from Jane. Worry clouded her thoughts, and she pressed her lips together unhappily.

Jane did not confide in her that night. The poor dear seemed to have gathered her misery about her like a cloak. She hid it well; her face was a mask of serene contentment. Elizabeth did not pry. She and Jane lay side by side, both silent, drifting off to sleep with none of the conversation they usually engaged in before retiring for the night.

The next day, Sally brought Elizabeth a letter, handing it to her with a little curtsey. The seal declared it to be from Mr. Darcy, and she hastily tucked it into her pocket, ignoring her aunt's probing looks. "It is from Charlotte," she said, lying brazenly to protect her secret. Aunt Gardiner seemed to accept that, and they returned to their mending, the missive burning conspicuously against Elizabeth's leg.

Finally, some time after tea, Elizabeth escaped to her shared bedchamber. Jane's occupation with their cousins gave Elizabeth some privacy to read the letter. Hastily, she broke the seal, cognizant that anyone could enter her chambers and interrupt.

My Dearest Miss Elizabeth,

I hope this letter finds you in good health, though I confess it brings with it both a sense of profound gratitude and an undeniable pang of guilt. Your words have reached me with such unexpected warmth and clarity that I find myself both overjoyed and deeply contrite about the way I have behaved. Indeed, I must first beg your forgiveness for the utter inconsistency of my actions and words, which, I now see, have caused you no small degree of confusion and distress.

Your candor, Miss Elizabeth, is a balm to my soul, and it is only by your gracious patience that I find the courage to speak plainly. The man you describe—proud, aloof, disdainful—is, I fear, a reflection of my own shortcomings, of my inability to express my true feelings in a way that might have spared you such unnecessary hurt. You are right to question the drastic change in my conduct, and I must confess that I have been struggling to understand how I arrived at such a place. My pride, my self-doubt, and a misguided sense of what was proper led me to suppress the very emotions that now overwhelm me.

When I last spoke with you in November, I was a fool—too proud and too blind to recognize the genuine affection I held for you. How I regret the words that have so wounded you, and how I long to undo the damage they have caused. But, alas, I cannot turn back time, and I am left only with the hope that you will see, through this letter, that my heart is not as it once was.

The pain I have spoken of in this letter is not unlike that which your sister, Jane, has suffered—though I must admit, in my case, it has been a pain borne not only of unspoken feelings but also of a great deal of self-loathing. I am not as guarded as I once believed; I am merely frightened—frightened that you would never look upon me with affection, that my faults would forever stand between us. But you, Miss Bennet, have shown me that love, when it is true, does not bow to pride or to circumstance. Your letter fills me with a hope that I had long abandoned. It seems as though, against all odds, you have found some measure of kindness in your heart for me, despite my previous shortcomings. I am in awe of your generosity and your wisdom.

I wish, with all my heart, that I could tell you how much I long to know more of you, to learn all that makes you the remarkable woman you are. Your words have brought me a glimpse of who is beneath the surface—the woman whose strength and honesty have so thoroughly captivated me. I desire, above all, to prove myself worthy of your trust, and to show you my love is unfeigned—a love that is as steadfast and true as you deserve.

Your assurance that mercenary thoughts do not motivate you humbles me. I never doubted your integrity, Miss Bennet, but it is a relief to know that we are of like minds in this regard. Wealth and status, once so important to me, now hold no claim on my heart. It is a shared understanding, mutual respect, and, yes, love that I seek. If I have any hope of winning your heart, I know it must be through sincerity and by showing you that my feelings are not fleeting or capricious, but enduring and deep.

I am pleased to hear you will be in London. The pain in my heart lessens knowing you are closer than before. I shall make every effort to meet with you at a time and place of your choosing, if you deem it appropriate. Should discretion be required, I shall ensure that all correspondence is placed directly into Sally's hands, as you so kindly suggested. I only wish to hear from you again, and to discover, together, what the future may hold.

With the deepest affection, and a heart full of hope,
Fitzwilliam Darcy

Elizabeth's face flushed as she read the letter, filled to bursting with new declarations of love and admiration. His apologies, so expertly tendered, went a long way to healing the hurt he had inflicted. Perhaps there was more to the enigmatic gentleman from the north than she had supposed. A sudden desire to pen her sentiments filled her, and she hastened to the little table by the window where her writing box stood. *There is no time to lose,* she told herself. As she prepared her paper, she marveled at how rapidly her sentiments had changed. The line between love and hate was indeed thin, and she had walked it precariously for longer than she realized.

Could I love him? she asked. It seemed very probable. Her heart, still undecided, leaned more towards him today than it had yesterday. She had no doubt that if Mr. Darcy continued to woo her with his well-written, romantic letters, she would be irrevocably gone before she knew what had occurred.

January 1812
Darcy House
Georgiana

"What is that?" Fitzwilliam appeared behind her, and she froze, the last letter from Elizabeth half unfolded in her hand. Although her hand obscured the impression, the seal faced upward. Had her brother seen it?

"Nothing!" she squeaked, her voice high-pitched and slightly frantic. "It is merely a letter from...from Eliza Wilson! Yes, she is a friend...from school!" Biting her lip to stop her rambling, Georgiana slowly lowered the letter to her lap and placed a hand over it. She could feel her cheeks flushing, testifying to the lie that spilled from her lips.

Her brother frowned. "I do not recall you mentioning such a person," he mused. "Is she a very close friend?"

Georgiana struggled to come up with an answer. "Close enough," she finally muttered.

Apparently satisfied, Fitzwilliam turned his attention back to his correspondence. "I do wish Bingley would write legibly," he muttered as he attempted to decipher his friend's writing.

"How is Mr. Bingley?" Georgiana asked. Elizabeth had mentioned him in her letters. Mr. Bingley had, according to her, abandoned her sister, Jane, leaving her heartbroken. Though Georgiana once thought very well of the gentleman, his disgraceful, capricious manner towards the eldest Miss Bennet had infuriated her. Did he not know how fragile a lady's heart was? *She* knew what it felt like to be discarded with little thought. *Poor Miss Bennet,* she thought for the hundredth time.

"He is tolerably well," Fitzwilliam replied, reminding Georgiana of the insult her brother had lobbed at Miss Elizabeth. She frowned. "He is in town. They spent the holidays in Surrey at Hurst's estate."

"Why do you say he is tolerable?" she asked innocently. Fitzwilliam glanced up at her for a moment, his lips twitching slightly as he observed her countenance, which she kept carefully blank.

"He suffered a disappointment in the autumn," he finally replied. "Another fortune hunting mama and her daughter tried to ensnare him."

Scoffing, Georgiana poked a bit of egg with her fork. "His sisters disapproved of the lady, did they not?" she asked bitterly.

Her brother looked up, surprise written on his face. "Yes, of course they did," he intoned. "She was entirely unsuitable." Seemingly content with that answer, Fitzwilliam speared another bite of food with his fork, putting it in his mouth and chewing slowly.

"How so?" Georgiana would not let it rest. Elizabeth had not accused Fitzwilliam of aiding in the separation, but she now suspected her brother indeed had something to do with Miss Bennet's heartbreak. If it was true, Elizabeth would not want the man who had ruined the happiness of a beloved sister.

"Their mother is from trade and as gauche and uncouth as any fishmonger's wife. The three youngest sisters have little sense and expose their family to ridicule at every turn. It would be a degradation for Bingley to marry into such a situation."

It all sounded very rehearsed. She recalled the letter she found—it *was* a recital! Fitzwilliam had likely cited these same reasons to himself many times. *So, you love one sister, and Bingley the other. Perhaps you removed your friend from temptation to protect yourself?* It was an interesting thought, and one worth considering.

"Mr. Bingley is from trade," she reminded him. "And Miss Bingley behaves like the worst sort of fortune hunter. How is that any different?" She kept her tone curious, struggling to hide the accusations that threatened to burst forth.

"It is hardly the same! The Bingley sisters behave properly amongst society—"

"Do they?" she cut in. "Have you heard Aunt Matlock complain about their pretensions?"

Fitzwilliam gaped. "Besides," she continued, "if you compare them by rank, the Bennets are higher placed in society than the Bingleys. They own an estate, and the Bennets have likely been gentry for many generations."

"Yes, Mr. Bennet is a gentleman," Fitzwilliam said slowly. "But who is Mrs. Bennet? Who are her relations?"

Georgiana looked up slowly. "Careful, Brother," she said evenly, "for you begin to sound very much like Lady Catherine." She watched smugly as the color drained from Fitzwilliam's face. He *hated* being compared to their aunt.

"I do not," he muttered.

She put her fork down. "I realize things like rank and fortune require some attention," she said softly. "What if I met a man with middling rank and a modest fortune? What if we loved each other truly—genuine, unfeigned love—would you deny me?"

"I see your point," Fitzwilliam said, his brow furrowing. "The Misses Bennet have no fortune and no rank, so it is very different. Their estate is entailed away—"

"But would not marrying Miss Bennet elevate Mr. Bingley?" she cried. "I know most would say *she* would be marrying down, and according to your explanations last summer, that is the truth of the matter! I do not understand why Mr. Bingley should not marry the lady if he loves her."

"He does love her." Fitzwilliam raised his voice slightly, a testament to his growing unease. "It is her feelings which are in doubt."

Finally, the crux of the matter. "Has he asked the lady if she cares for him?" she asked. "A *proper* lady is not supposed to show what she feels until a gentleman declares himself."

Frowning, he shook his head. "Bingley was persuaded to quit the area," he said. "I saw no evidence of Miss Bennet's affections. Indeed, it seemed as though her mother would press her to accept the first wealthy man who offered. Bingley saw the logic and accepted the facts as I presented them."

Georgiana knew differently, but she could say nothing. If Elizabeth's mother was of that ilk, then she would now be married to her father's heir. Yet, she was in London and unwed. "The facts as *you* presented them?" she repeated. "Oh, Fitzwilliam, did you interfere?"

"Marriage is not a game, Georgiana," he scolded. "I would not see my friend tied to someone who married him only for his fortune! He would be miserable."

"*You* would be miserable in a similar relationship," she quipped. "Be that as it may, I do not understand why you are the authority on Miss Bennet's feelings. It is not for you to determine the nature of her sentiments—that is Mr. Bingley's responsibility. What if you were in error?"

"I was not," he said, but she could hear the doubt in his voice. "She smiles at everyone...there was no sign!" He looked slightly concerned, his brow furrowed as he regarded his plate seriously.

"And if you were? What are the consequences for Miss Bennet? A lady's reputation is a fragile thing, something easily ruined. It is a lesson I was forced to learn last summer." *That is enough prodding,* she thought. Carefully, she put her fork down and stood, excusing herself.

"When did you grow so wise?" her brother murmured as she drifted past. Making no reply, Georgiana hurried to the salver, hoping to find a letter waiting on it.

January 1812
Darcy House
Georgiana

The butler, Mr. Smith, held the stack in his hand. "I will take those!" she cried, hurrying forward. The butler looked bemused but did not protest. He handed the stack to his mistress and bowed slightly before striding away. A quick glance through the missives revealed one from Miss Elizabeth addressed to her brother.

"That was too close," she muttered. She would have to be more careful. The time approached when she would need to tell her brother of her deceit, but hopefully it would not come until Miss Elizabeth was in love with him. Hurrying to her room, she locked herself in and tore open the letter.

My Dear Mr. Darcy,

Your letter, though it reached me with the weight of a thousand emotions, has not caused me the distress you fear, but rather, a softening of my heart. I had not expected such a thoughtful and sincere response, and yet, I find myself moved by your words in a way I did not believe possible.

First, let me assure you, sir, that I do not hold your past conduct against you—at least, not with the bitterness that might have been expected. It seems to me that you have, in fact, found a better path, one that is less dominated by pride and more by reflection. To hear you acknowledge your previous misjudgments with such candor and humility is not only a rare thing to witness, but one that speaks to the integrity of your character. It is not easy to acknowledge one's own faults, and I admire your courage in doing so.

While your words last autumn wounded me more than I could express at the time, I cannot help but understand them in light of your current feelings. You speak of self-loathing and fear, and though I cannot condone the manner in which they were expressed, I see they were born not of malice but of the confusion and uncertainty that often accompany matters of the heart. I, too, have felt such confusion, and I believe we have both been more blind to our own affections than we would care to admit.

You say that your pride and self-doubt have kept you from seeing the truth of your feelings until now. Perhaps, sir, it is the same pride that has made me so cautious and reluctant to acknowledge the stirrings of affection that your letter has stirred within my heart. In truth, that fickle organ, which was once resolved against you finds itself torn between surprise and hope. There is a vulnerability in your words that I cannot deny; it touches me deeply, and it makes me wonder if we, too, may have more in common than I ever imagined.

As for my sister Jane, I must confess that until recently I had not thought to draw a parallel between her and you, but it now seems so apparent. Her own struggles with love and the hidden depths of her feelings have often mirrored my own, though less apparent to those observing her, and I see now that I may have been too quick to dismiss the idea that someone such as you could feel with such depth. I do not claim to fully understand your heart, Mr. Darcy, but I will admit that I am intrigued—perhaps even more than I should be.

Your words concerning wealth and status are, I believe, as sincere as the rest of your sentiments, and they assure me we are indeed of like minds. You are not the man I first thought you to be, nor am I the woman I was when I first judged you so harshly. The way forward, I trust, will not be without difficulty or misunderstanding, but it seems to me that we now find ourselves on a path that could lead to something far more meaningful than either of us had expected.

The tone of this letter is far too heavy for me, sir, and so I shall now ask for more personal details—your likes and dislikes, passions and pursuits. To begin, let me inquire what your favorite color and treat are. As I picture you in my mind, I see staid Mr. Darcy partaking of fruit cake. Your preferred hue I dare not speculate—I have never beheld you in anything but black. Be so good as to satisfy my curiosity!

As to meeting in London, I would be happy to do so, though I trust we will proceed with caution, as you suggest. The mere thought of being able to converse with you freely feels strange, for I never imagined a time when I would seek you out for discussion. I must admit that I am still unsure as to what the future holds. It would be foolish to pretend that everything is settled between us, but I am willing, Mr. Darcy, to explore where this unexpected connection may lead.

You have, without a doubt, earned my respect, and for that, I am grateful. As for my feelings, I dare not claim certainty, but I am open to discovering, alongside you, what might be possible.

I remain, with sincerity and a heart uncertain yet hopeful,
Elizabeth Bennet

Georgiana sighed. "Oh, each letter is better than the last!" she cried. "I can see why Fitzwilliam fell in love with her." She would need to compose a reply, and soon. Each letter took a very long time to compose and copy to new paper. Writing in a script similar to her brother's became easier with each missive, though the process was still arduous.

Taking a sheet of paper out, Georgiana paused before writing. The information she gained that morning could be ruinous to her brother's future. Mr. Bingley was not happy to be away from his love. Perhaps she could do something about that. Putting aside her task, she decided to interfere with yet another romance.

In thick, block letters, she wrote.

Dear Sir,

I trust this letter finds you in good health. I find myself in possession of information that, though it may cause you some surprise, could very well benefit you in matters of the heart. Though I would not speak lightly of such things, there are times when a few words of truth, however indirect, may serve to clear the air and offer some much-needed guidance.

It is with this in mind that I pen this note. The hopes of last autumn, I believe, have not been in vain, though they may have seemed distant in the time that has passed. Rest assured, sir, the lady in question holds you in the deepest regard. She loves you, though she has carefully concealed her feelings beneath the calm facade she has so assiduously maintained. I assure you, this is no mark of indifference or insincerity, but rather the proper conduct of a lady who, as you know, must guard her emotions—and reputation—with the utmost care. Do not be too harsh in your judgment of her actions, for her restraint has been borne of necessity, not of disregard for your affections.

I cannot pretend to know the full depths of her heart, but I am certain that she has long held you in esteem. Her manner, perhaps, may have led you to believe otherwise, but I ask you to consider the possibility that the mask she wears is not one of indifference, but of modesty and caution, as befitting her station.

Should you find it in your heart to pursue this matter, there is a place where you may seek her. If you love Miss Jane Bennet, you can find her at 27 Gracechurch Street. I cannot say more, for the particulars of such things are better left for you to discover. But I trust you will understand that this small bit of direction is offered with the sincerest of intentions.

Know that I am but a friend, one who has observed, and perhaps understands, more than is readily apparent. What you do with this information is entirely your own affair, but I hope it may guide you towards a favorable outcome.

Yours sincerely,

A Friend

Smiling smugly, she sanded and folded the missive, dropping a blob of wax onto the paper to seal it. She wrote the direction in similar block lettering before entrusting it to her maid, who was always discreet. "See this into Mr. Bingley's hands," she said. No one in that household knew her maid's face, thus protecting Georgiana from discovery.

Satisfied, she pulled a fresh sheet of paper towards her. She needed to complete the letter to Elizabeth soon.

January 1812
Gracechurch Street
Elizabeth

"Mr. Bingley!" Jane's surprise was written on her face and in her words. Her pleasure, though, could not be contained, and her face brightened considerably, her mouth spreading into a wide smile. "Welcome, sir! I had not thought to see you whilst I was in town."

"I knew of your presence only yesterday," he admitted. "A rather strange note arrived...but I digress. I have missed your company very much, Miss Bennet. And yours, too, Miss Elizabeth. Of course."

Aunt Gardiner raised an eyebrow at the gentleman as Jane performed introductions. Feeling rather *de trop*, Elizabeth retreated to a corner, content to stitch away at her embroidery whilst the young couple reunited in peace. Her aunt joined her, leaning towards her to speak in low tones.

"His sisters lied," she said. "They told us their brother was much occupied with Miss Darcy."

"Yes, Miss Bingley wrote the same to Jane when they quit Netherfield. I did not believe it." Mr. Bingley's affection for Jane was so obvious. So, too, was her sister's. Having been in depressed spirits for some time, it seemed Jane had no energy to maintain her serene mask. Happiness radiated out of her. The love and admiration on her countenance could not be mistaken.

Love unfeigned. The words she and Mr. Darcy had exchanged resounded in her head. It had been a few days since she received another missive. She wanted a letter to arrive and felt anxious with each day that went by. A thought struck her. The primary purpose for engaging in clandestine correspondence was now resolved. Jane was reunited with Mr. Bingley. There was no need to continue the pretense of caring for Mr. Darcy.

Pretense? No, it was not a pretense. Elizabeth forced herself to admit that her heart was now engaged. Mr. Darcy's tender affection could not be mistaken. Her own feelings were now inextricably linked to that gentleman, despite her previous sentiments. If he ceased writing, she would be heartbroken.

Sally appeared at her side, offering Mrs. Gardiner a few letters before handing one to Elizabeth. The handwriting was instantly recognizable, and she hid the letter in her pocket before her aunt questioned who the sender might be. Feeling happier than she had in a few days, Elizabeth hummed as she stitched.

Mr. Bingley stayed an hour, promising to return on the morrow. Jane, now blushing with happiness, gave him an ardent farewell. When he had gone, she turned to Elizabeth and Mrs. Gardiner. "Is it possible to die of happiness?" she cried. Tears fell, and she collapsed onto the settee, sobs wracking her body. "I thought I had lost him forever," she said, the sorrow she had suppressed for months spilling forth. "It is all well now. He did not know I was in town!"

"Those two harpies likely concealed your presence," Aunt Gardiner huffed.

"That is likely the most unforgiving thing I have ever heard you utter," Elizabeth chuckled. "I believe I shall go upstairs." Pausing, she kissed her sister's head. "I am very happy for you, Jane."

Safely in her chambers, she sat near the window, breaking the seal to the letter and reading what Mr. Darcy had written.

My Dearest Miss Elizabeth,

I hope this letter finds you in the best of health and good spirits. Please accept my apologies for the delay in my response; a few pressing matters of business, though not nearly as delightful as our correspondence, have occupied my time. I trust you have not found my silence too burdensome and that, as ever, you are in good health and enjoying the peace that you deserve.

Now that I have cleared away the misunderstandings of our past, which I trust we may consider well behind us, I find myself wishing to speak of more pleasant things. I confess, Miss Elizabeth, that I have told you very little of myself, and as you have shown a surprising degree of curiosity, which I cannot help but find most endearing, I now feel it is time to remedy that deficiency.

As you know, I have a sister—Georgiana. She is sixteen, and, as I am certain you will agree, the very soul of sweetness and propriety. While Miss Bingley may speak of her musical accomplishments with an air of informed interest, her opinions hardly matter. I can assure you that my sister fills Pemberley with music and light. Her talent on the pianoforte and her voice—her sweet, angelic voice!—they are the very heart of our home. It has often struck me that the quiet grandeur of Pemberley, with its vast, echoing halls, feels somewhat lonely without her music. Georgiana's notes, so bright and pure, are the melody to which the house beats, and it is only in the sound of her playing that the silence is lifted.

As a sister, she is all I could have wished for—gracious, gentle, and, above all, kind. She has come through many trials, not the least of which was last summer. You must know—surely you must understand—that Georgiana's heart is tender, and last year she suffered a disappointment that has left her somewhat shaken. I will not trouble you with all the details, but suffice it to say that she placed her trust in a gentleman whom we had long known and who was, I regret to say, unworthy of that trust. His behavior towards her has caused no small amount of distress, and it has taken Georgiana some time to recover her confidence.

This gentleman, this blackguard, has gone his own way, and I have no wish to speak of him further. I would not waste another breath on a man who has dishonored the very name of Darcy. He has no claim on my goodwill, nor on my sister's heart, which she has withdrawn from him forever. The breach caused by his actions is beyond repair, and I cannot say enough how deeply I despise him for the pain he caused her. Yet, despite her sorrow, I am pleased to report that Georgiana is doing better now—though she recovers slowly, she is far more at ease than she was some months ago. It seems that the kind attention of her family, and the encouragement of those who love her, has restored some of her spirits.

But now, to lighten the tone and make myself more agreeable, I believe it is time to indulge you with some of those mundane questions I suspect you have been so patiently awaiting. I shall begin by answering your own, as I have often wondered whether you, too, have such preferences as I do. You asked, I believe, of my favorite color and treat. To begin with, I am partial to blue. There is something about the color that soothes the mind and evokes a sense of calm, do you not think? As for my treat of choice, be aware that I do not like fruit cake at all—I am ever partial to lemon tarts. Their tart sweetness never fails to brighten my mood, and I dare say I could indulge in them far too often if I were not careful.

And now to present you with a question of my own, and my answer. Do you have a favorite animal, Miss Elizabeth? I confess a fondness for dogs over cats, though I have neither at present. My hunting dogs are the closest companions I have in this regard, and I have always preferred the more affectionate sort. I am told I may be too fond of them—though I am certain you would not judge me harshly for it.

And now, I must ask in return—what are your own tastes? I can hardly imagine you with a color preference that would not match your wit and charm, nor can I imagine what treat would be worthy of your refined tastes. I must confess, I am curious, though I am certain I shall be surprised—though, as you know, I have long since learned not to underestimate you.

I look forward to hearing your thoughts on these simple matters. Perhaps they shall bring a smile to your face, as I hope they have to mine.

With the utmost affection and sincere admiration,
Fitzwilliam Darcy

Elizabeth caressed the letter, sighing happily. "Cats are infinitely preferable to dogs," she said aloud. "I shall have to teach you that, sir!" With anticipation of another response, she composed a reply, her heart becoming more his with every word.

January 1812
Darcy House
Georgiana

F itzwilliam let out a cry as he spilled his cup of tea. "What the devil!" he cried. "My apologies, Georgiana."

She looked up in surprise. "What happened?" she asked. "Have you received some unpleasant news?"

Fitzwilliam shook his head. She could see his hand quiver as he turned the missive in his hand over. "It is only a very unexpected letter," he said. "It is from a lady. I am unsure if I ought to open it or consign it to the fire. It is highly improper for her to have written to an unmarried gentleman."

Her heart sank, and she felt the color drain from her face. "Do not throw it away!" she cried. "Please! It is my fault. Oh, you will be so angry when I tell you!" Georgiana said as she burst into tears. She buried her head in her hands. *How had the post come early that day?* she wondered. It rarely arrived until after breakfast. Now everything was on the cusp of falling to pieces.

Her brother came to her side and placed a comforting hand on her shoulder. "Tell me what has happened, dearest," he said quietly. "I promise I shall not be angry."

"You cannot say that," she sniffed, looking up. "You may very well hate me for what I have done!" In halting speech, she described her actions, detailing how she had painstakingly learned to imitate his script and sent love letters on his behalf. "I did it for your own good!" she said as she finished. "You were miserable. I wanted to make it better. But that letter you penned was atrocious."

Her brother sat beside her, his face an unreadable mask. "What did you say to her?" he asked quietly.

"I have copies of the letters," she confessed. "I kept the originals—they were very well crafted, if I do say so myself."

"Go get them," he commanded. His voice did not sound sharp, but she hastened to obey, nonetheless. It was quick work to retrieve them—and Elizabeth's replies—from the box in the back of the wardrobe where she had hidden them. Once returned to the parlor, she handed the stack to her brother.

"That is everything," she said. "Can I open the new letter?"

"No!" he snapped. "I must ascertain how much damage has been done and come up with a plan to mitigate it. My honor is likely engaged—Georgiana, you have decided my entire future! I must think." Fitzwilliam stood and left the room, closing the door behind him. Appetite gone, she stayed where she was, sorrow and fear crashing over her in waves.

What have I done?

Darcy

He held the letters in his hand. There were quite a few—how long had his sister been writing to Miss Elizabeth in his stead? Darcy arranged the missives by the dates at the top of each, with the newest at the back. He stood and went to the door, locking it so he would not be disturbed.

It took him some time to read each one. Georgiana had done a credible job of imitating him. Every letter contained the sentiments he wished to say to Elizabeth for months, and written so eloquently. He would not have expected it of his baby sister, but here they were. Elizabeth's replies were surprising, too. He gathered her feelings had undergone a metamorphosis of some kind—had she truly disliked him? He had seen no indication of it in Hertfordshire. Indeed, he thought she had been flirting with him.

Suddenly, Georgiana's prodding about marrying for love made sense. She knew it would all come to light eventually and had worked to soften him to the idea before it did. *How long did she mean to carry this out before revealing everything?* he wondered. One letter spoke of meeting, but nothing had been arranged. *Surely, before* that *took place.*

Another thought struck him. Bingley and his relationship with Miss Jane Bennet now filled his mind. If he had so misunderstood Elizabeth's feelings, then had he also mistaken her sister's? "Oh, what have I done?" Despite her unsuitability in terms of wealth and connections, Darcy would have had no objection to the lady if she held genuine affection for his friend. Marrying a gently born lady *would* aid Bingley in society.

Elizabeth's letters confirmed his folly. Miss Bennet suffered from a broken heart, and it was his fault. He knew, of course, of her presence in town, but had attributed it to the brazen attempts of a matchmaking lady stalking her prey. He had encouraged the Bingley sisters to delay returning the call so Miss Bennet would be in no doubt that the acquaintance was at an end.

"I must make it right," he muttered. Putting the letters aside, he immediately penned a note to Bingley.

Bingley,

I was wrong. Miss Bennet loves you. She stays with her aunt and uncle on Gracechurch Street. Go to her as soon as you can. Come to Darcy House for an explanation later.

FD

It was hastily done and had as many blots as one of Bingley's own letters, but it would have to do. He sent it with a footman directly, hoping his friend would not hate him for his sins.

Returning to the letters, he opened the last one. He wanted to know what Elizabeth had to say, how she would reply to his—Georgiana's, rather—latest missive. Despite his anger at his sister, he had greatly enjoyed perusing the correspondence she had exchanged with Miss Elizabeth Bennet. If anything, each word had pulled him more into the lady's thrall. He loved her more now than he had an hour before. Anticipation mounting, he broke the seal.

My Dearest Mr. Darcy,

I trust this letter finds you in excellent health and good spirits. Your previous correspondence, which arrived with such delightful and unexpected warmth, has caused me no small amount of amusement. I confess that your reflections on Pemberley's silence, filled only by your sister's music, painted a picture that I found both charming and evocative. Miss Darcy's sweet melodies echoing through the halls, much like a voice calling to the very soul of the house, bringing life to its quiet corners, is a sight I can imagine with clarity. I must confess that I now find myself rather wishing to hear them for myself, though I am certain I could not do justice to such a talented performer as your sister.

How very kind you are to share with me such intimate details of your sister's trials. I am deeply touched by the affection you clearly have for her, and the gentleness with which you regard her disappointment. How cruelly the heart can be deceived by those we trust! I am so sorry to hear that she suffered such a betrayal, but I am heartened to know she is recovering. It is no small comfort to know that, with you as her brother, she has the steadfast support of someone so capable and caring. I can only hope that, with time, Miss Darcy will regain the confidence that has been so undeservedly shaken.

As for your questions of my own preferences, I will not keep you in suspense any longer. I must admit, I am rather fond of the color green—it is, to my eye, the color of new beginnings, of life in full bloom, and it always reminds me of the countryside. Perhaps that is not quite so surprising, given that I have always loved the outdoors. As for treats, I find myself partial to a good apple tart, especially when served warm, with a dollop of cream. There is something about its sweetness and simplicity that appeals to me, and I dare say I could eat more than my share if I were not careful.

As for animals, I must confess that I have never had the pleasure of owning either a dog or a cat, though I am rather partial to the idea of the latter. There is something familiar about the animal's mischievous behavior, I believe. I imagine I would enjoy the quiet companionship of a cat very well, though perhaps I would not trust it as implicitly as I would a dog.

I must tell you, Mr. Darcy, that it is rather delightful to share such trivial preferences with you. In our usual exchanges, I often find myself lost in deeper matters, but this, I dare say, is a welcome diversion. I look forward to hearing more of your thoughts on the simpler things in life, though I must admit that my curiosity about your deeper feelings for your family, and particularly for Miss Darcy, has not abated.

I trust that this letter, though lighter in tone than our previous ones, finds you in good humor. I must thank you again for your sincerity and your kindness, which I find more endearing with each passing day. It is a rare pleasure to be on such familiar terms with a man of your discernment, and I treasure these exchanges more than I can quite express. Beyond those sentiments, I must impart that I long to meet you in person. May it be soon.

With the greatest respect and fondest regard,
Elizabeth Bennet

He closed the letter slowly. *I love her,* he thought. *Most ardently.* He knew in an instant that no amount of distance would have cured him of the ailment. Elizabeth Bennet was the only woman he had ever felt any measure of affection for, and at eight-and-twenty, he doubted he would ever feel the same for another more suitable woman.

She is my match in every way, he thought. *And I almost lost her.* Georgiana made it seem so easy, but now perhaps it was. His honor was thoroughly engaged, and marriage was the only way to ensure it remained intact. Instead of being furious at his sister, he suddenly felt grateful for her interference. The choice which he had wrestled with for so many months had been made for him.

Sitting before his writing desk, he pulled a paper towards him to begin his reply. He wanted to meet Elizabeth, to see her in person. As he dipped his pen into ink, his confidence failed him. *What am I to say?* Feeling chagrined, he rang for Georgiana. She had got him into this mess, and now she would help him compose a proper missive to his lady love.

January 1812
Gracechurch Street
Elizabeth

Elizabeth's latest letter came far sooner than she had anticipated. There were usually two or three days between missives, even when she replied immediately upon receiving one. This pleased her, and she took advantage of the particularly fine day to read her letter in the little park down the street from her aunt's house.

The cold months were not over yet. January always seemed long and dreary. The uncharacteristically bright sky cheered her and reminded Elizabeth that spring was only a few weeks away. She walked briskly; despite the sun, it was still chilly, and her speed worked to push away the chill. Soon she entered the park gate and made her way to a little bench she knew stood amidst the bare trees. It was secluded in the summer months, but the lack of foliage left it more open to the surrounding area.

Elizabeth settled on the bench, the stone like ice despite the layers of skirts and outerwear she wore. Her gloves made her fumble as she broke the seal on Mr. Darcy's letter. Humming happily, she began to read.

My Dearest Miss Elizabeth,

Your letter, as ever, arrives as a source of great pleasure. It is a rare gift indeed, to find one so perfectly capable of blending humor with sincerity, and wisdom with light-heartedness. I confess, I found myself smiling as I read your reflections on Georgiana's music, and I would be delighted for you to hear her play in person. I shall, of course, leave you to be the judge of whether her talent is equal to Miss Bingley's exclamations, though I imagine, should you grace us with your presence, you would find a way to do so most kindly, as always.

Your compassion for my sister moves me more than I can express. It is true that her heart was deeply wounded by the actions of someone she had come to trust, and though I would never have wished such a trial upon her, it is a comfort to know she has so many who care for her well-being. I have no doubt that with time, her spirits will mend, and I hope to see her, once again, filled with the lively confidence I know she is capable of. Your kindness in acknowledging her pain gives me hope she might one day find solace in the company of such a strong and understanding woman as yourself.

Your response to my questions of preference has, as always, captured my interest. How fascinating it is to hear that you favor the color green—an association I shall now forever attach to you, as it seems so fitting. Green, the color of life and renewal, and of someone who has always seen the world with an eye for its possibilities. I must admit that I too find the color pleasing, though my fondness for blue has never quite been eclipsed. As for apple tarts, I must say your taste in desserts does you great credit. There is something most comforting about the simplicity of a well-made pastry, especially when shared in pleasant company. I do hope, should we meet, we might share such a treat, though I suspect, knowing my own weaknesses, I would be quite tempted to take the larger portion.

As for your preference for cats, I must confess that I too find them charming in their mischievousness. Their independent nature, their quiet attentions, have always fascinated me. Though, I agree, there is something reassuring about the loyalty of a dog—perhaps that is a trait I hold in higher esteem than I should, but I trust you will allow me this small indulgence. A dog, for me, is a companion who offers a constant, unspoken understanding, even when words fail. I should imagine, though, that you, Miss Elizabeth, would possess a way of speaking to both animals and people alike, that leaves them quite content to be in your presence.

It warms my heart that you enjoy these more mundane exchanges as much as I do. For as much as our conversations have traversed deeper matters, there is a certain joy in these simple diversions, in learning about one another's tastes and preferences. Indeed, I look forward to hearing more, as I feel it reveals as much about the heart as any profound discourse could.

And now, I must take a moment to share how pleased I am that you have expressed a desire to meet in person. It is a sentiment that I share but have hesitated to speak aloud. The opportunity to speak with you face-to-face, to see the spark in your eyes as you express yourself so freely and without any reserve, is enticing indeed. I have no doubt that such a meeting would be most rewarding, and I can only hope that we might arrange it soon. There are so many things I wish to say, and I find that my heart is full with the thought of sharing them with you.

With the deepest affection and the highest regard,
Fitzwilliam Darcy

Closing the letter, Elizabeth already began composing her reply in her head. She had many questions she wished to ask and enumerated them as she held the missive in her hand. A little voice in her head reminded her of Mr. Darcy's treatment of Mr. Wickham, but she dismissed it entirely. She had, after receiving the news of Georgiana's disappointment at the hand of a friend, speculated that this was the source of the rift between Mr. Darcy and the scarlet-coated officer. Even if Mr. Wickham was not involved, the speculations had caused her to revisit her memories of the man's recitations. In doing so, she found many inconsistencies and began to doubt that he spoke the truth of the situation.

Returning to her aunt's house, Elizabeth hid the letters at the bottom of her writing chest beneath the velvet lining that had come loose years ago. It was bulging—she would have to find another place to conceal her illicit correspondence.

After securing the treasured bit of paper, she returned to the sitting room where her aunt and Jane awaited her. Mr. Bingley would arrive soon. He had plans to accompany them to Bond Street. Elizabeth felt great excitement. Beyond ordering two new gowns, she wished to visit Hatchard's. The novels she brought with her from Longbourn had been read and she wished to acquire something new to read.

"Back from your stroll?" Aunt Gardiner asked, amused. "I wondered how long you would resist. Though you hate the cold, you dislike being confined indoors more."

"How well you know me, Aunt!" Elizabeth grinned. "The air was brisk, but my walk was rejuvenating! I am ready to be poked and prodded as we are measured for new gowns."

The ladies laughed together. Elizabeth liked new clothing as much as the next lady, but she disliked being required to stand still for any amount of time. Their laughs turned to chuckles as the front bell rang, and they turned eagerly to greet Mr. Bingley.

"Good day to you all!" He came forward and bowed low over Jane's hand, placing a chaste kiss on its back. "You look beautiful, Miss Bennet," he said earnestly.

"Thank you, sir." Jane blushed a pretty pink. "You look very fine as well. I do so admire you in blue."

Mr. Bingley had wasted no time in requesting a courtship. After an interrogation by their uncle, the gentleman had been granted leave to call upon Jane. He made an appearance every day at Gracechurch Street now, his attentions more marked than ever before. Elizabeth gave him a week before he proposed.

Jane could not stop smiling. Her worn, drawn face had transformed, and the love she felt for Mr. Bingley made her more beautiful than ever. She radiated happiness, and her appearance shifted into something more stunning. No one could doubt her feelings now.

They left the house and boarded a respectable carriage. There were rugs to ward off the chill, and the plush cushions were comfortable. Mr. Bingley chattered away as the coach trundled along. Jane and Mrs. Gardiner listened raptly, but Elizabeth's mind wandered as she stared out the window, her thoughts on Mr. Darcy and the tender feelings for the man that were budding within her.

She did not dare dream of a future with him. It seemed like a fairy tale—men of his consequence did not marry the daughters of insignificant country gentlemen. Mr. Bingley was the son of a tradesman. Wealthy or not, his social standing was closer to Jane's than Elizabeth's was to Mr. Darcy's.

He is a gentleman. I am a gentleman's daughter, she told herself. *In this, we are equal.* Her words reassured her only a little. *I shall feel better when I see him.* But when that would be, she did not know. He seemed to be leaving the decision in her hands.

Was she ready? She did not know. The last time they had been in company, they had exchanged words. She had accused him of ungentlemanly behavior, and he had responded coldly in that stiff, severe manner he often employed. The memory made her blush in shame—oh, how she had misjudged him!

They arrived at Bond Street, and Aunt Gardiner led them to Madame Dubois' Premiere Modiste Shoppe. Elizabeth knew it to be a more exclusive shop, frequented by ladies of the *ton* and looked at her aunt in question.

As it so happened, Aunt Gardiner had made friends with the shop proprietress. "It is worth it to befriend those who purchase my husband's wares," she said mischievously.

After an hour of being measured and selecting gowns, Elizabeth finally convinced her aunt to allow her to go to Hatchard's. The bookshop was three doors down. "Take Jones with you," Aunt Gardiner directed.

Pleased to be done with the modiste shop, Elizabeth agreed and left with the footman.

January 1812
Bond Street
Darcy

"What say you to visiting Bond Street today?" Darcy asked Georgiana. His letter had been dispatched to Gracechurch Street, and now he felt restless and confined. "I could do with a new book."

"Have you read the four you purchased last week?" Georgiana smirked. Darcy's penchant for purchasing more books than he could consume in a lifetime was well known. Her tease was an ongoing one—Darcy's father had said the same thing. He had added many tomes to the collection in his London house in the past few years. Darcy could not resist a good book. He read voraciously, and his interests covered a broad spectrum.

"Of course I have not," he said, winking at her. "Perhaps they have new music. You have played the same Mozart piece a million times now, if I had to guess."

His sister stuck her tongue out. "I have not," she denied. "But I should be pleased to join you. We have not ventured out for a few days."

It had been more than a few days. Darcy thought back, wondering when he had last taken Georgiana anywhere. He had brooded since the end of November when he had returned to London from Hertfordshire. Despite attending a few events over the holiday season, he had kept largely to himself, struggling to put the dark-haired beauty from his mind. His success had been limited.

The carriage was called, and they departed. Georgiana bounced with excitement, asking if they could visit the haberdashery whilst they were out. Darcy groaned dramatically but agreed, pleased to give his sister whatever she desired.

Her behavior had not gone unpunished. Darcy had scolded her severely, pressing upon her how her actions could have ruined his life. "What if I had decided I only felt infatuated?" he demanded. "What if Elizabeth did not like me, and she was forced to marry me because of the letter you sent? You could have ruined two lives, Georgie. It was badly done."

She had wept, and with tears streaming down her cheeks, apologized. "There is no harm done now, is there?" she asked meekly. "Elizabeth does not despise you, and I have overcome most of the obstacles that stood in your way."

"In a manner of speaking," he said, still frowning. "There is still the matter of her position in society. I am expected to make a brilliant match with a diamond of the first water."

Georgiana had frowned. "If you think Elizabeth is anything *but* the gem that she is, then you do not deserve her." She folded her arms petulantly. "Besides, you always wanted a marriage of affection—like Mama and Papa had. And now you will have it."

"There is no guarantee I would have met and fallen in love with a lady of the *ton*," he concurred. "And I have had it ingrained in me—these expectations for my marriage and future life will not be so easily set aside by our relations."

"Who cares what Lady Catherine thinks?" grumbled his sister. Georgiana tossed her hair, looking so much like Lydia Bennet in that instant that he swallowed hard.

"It is not just Lady Catherine," he said. "What about Aunt and Uncle Matlock?"

"Our aunt has been pressing you and our cousins to marry for years. She will be so relieved you are settling down that she will make no argument for fear of causing you to change your mind."

Darcy was forced to see his sister's point. "When did you become a studier of character?" he asked, bemused by her logic.

Georgiana had made no reply, merely staring at him triumphantly.

The carriage arrived in front of Hatchard's, and brother and sister climbed down. Darcy offered his arm to his sister, and they entered the store. The smell of books immediately assaulted his senses, and he breathed deeply. The scent was soothing to his soul, and some of the tension he carried around his shoulders eased.

"Good day, sir!" The proprietor nodded his head in greeting.

Darcy returned it, and he and Georgiana separated. She went to the music, and he walked down the long rows of books in search of something new to read. Near the end of the shelves, he spotted a lady in the next row over. His heart jumped to his throat as he recognized her.

Elizabeth. He moved as if under some unknown power. She stood on her tiptoes, her delicate fingertips attempting to retrieve a book on the top shelf.

"Almost there," he heard her hiss under her breath. She was so focused on what she was doing that she did not see him.

He reached up and plucked the book off the shelf and offered it to her. Elizabeth turned, her smile broad, and he watched with amusement as her words of gratitude died on her lips.

"Oh," she breathed, her cheeks flushing red. "Mr. Darcy." Elizabeth dipped a shallow curtsey and then bit her lip.

"Good day, Miss Elizabeth," Darcy replied huskily. "I did not expect to meet you so soon."

She looked up and the mischievous twinkle he so admired flashed in her eyes. "Yes, you have left that matter up to me, have you not? Should I hurry away and delay our meeting longer?"

"Minx," he said quietly. "No, I prefer you here." He reached out and drew a finger down her cheek. "It has been agony," he choked out as his hand dropped.

She reached out and took his hand in one of hers, squeezing it lightly. "I concur, sir. I have not had the opportunity to respond to your letter. We departed soon after I read it." Her cheeks reddened again, and she smiled shyly.

Darcy's throat felt dry. He realized now how different that look was from what she had leveled at him at Netherfield. "You really did not like me, did you?" he said, his voice, though quiet, sounding rather strangled.

"It is all forgotten," she said soothingly. "I did not know you. Indeed, I never knew myself until your first letter. How blurred the lines between lo—affection—and hate have been."

He heard her slip. *She loves me.* He longed to tell her how she affected him, how her very presence made it easier to breathe. He wanted her by his side forever. But now was not the time. He needed time to arrange his words in his head. Writing had always been the easiest way to express his feelings, though he had struggled with what to say in the last letter he had sent. His proposal needed to be perfect.

The bell at the door rang, informing them of another's entrance. Elizabeth backed away, putting a proper amount of space between them. A man approached—a footman, maybe?

"Miss Lizzy, your aunt says it is time to go."

"Thank you, Jones." Elizabeth turned to Mr. Darcy. "Farewell, sir."

"Goodbye." *Elizabeth*. He named her in his head. She went to the counter and paid for her book. Darcy trailed after her, a smitten look on his face. The bell jingled again as she departed, yet he remained rooted to where he stood.

"Brother?" Georgiana's words made him jump, and he turned to look at his sister. "Did you know that lady?" she asked. "I saw you watching her."

"That is Elizabeth," he said.

Georgiana's mouth opened in an 'O.' She beamed and then sighed with regret. "And I did not even get to meet her," she grumbled.

"Soon, dearest," he said. "Soon."

January 1812
Darcy House
Darcy

"Mr. Bingley to see you, sir." Darcy's butler stepped aside to allow the caller into the study.

"Good day, Darcy! How do you do?" Bingley looked happier than he had in months. His grin spread wide across his cheeks, which were pink from the cold. Bingley approached the desk almost swaggering, and Darcy wondered if he had met another angel—or perhaps he had seen Miss Bennet.

"Good day to you," he said, returning the greeting. "You seem in fine form this afternoon."

"Of course I am!" Bingley sat in the seat in front of Darcy's desk. "I have just returned from calling upon Jane—Miss Bennet, that is. Her aunt and uncle have a charming house. Very hospitable, the Gardiners."

Darcy nodded. "Yes, about Miss Bennet... Bingley, I am sorry. I thought I was advising you in the best way."

"No matter. By the time you sent your note, I already knew Jane was in town and had called upon the Gardiners to see her. I am very grateful she did not send me away with a flea in my ear. She had every right. One ought not to comment on a lady's appearance in an uncomplimentary fashion, but she looked dreadful. Eyes sunk in, expression morose..." Bingley trailed off. He looked ashamed. "I ought to have returned to Hertfordshire," he muttered, almost as if speaking to himself. "I knew she loved me, but I was a coward."

"She has forgiven you?" Darcy could only hope. Bingley would hate him forever if his best friend had cost him the love of his life.

Bingley nodded. "Yes! Jane is the most forgiving creature ever to live! I am very thankful she is so kindhearted. My honor was engaged—I see that now. One does not pay such attentions to a lady and then hie off to town with nary a word to her! Disgraceful."

His friend's wish to take responsibility for his actions impressed Darcy. Too often Bingley had leaned on others, relying on them to make important decisions. It was a habit that had crippled him for a long time. One cannot grow if one is too scared to take risks and make mistakes. Life was a messy business. No one could avoid slipping in the muck once in a while.

"You said you already received a note?" Darcy recalled his friend's words. "From whom?"

"I cannot tell you. It was written in big, blocky letters and signed, 'a friend.'" Bingley shrugged. "Whoever they are, I wish I could thank them. They did me a good turn—I will not forget it."

Darcy had his suspicions. Georgiana's pointed questions about Bingley and Miss Bennet and *his* interference were recalled to his mind. Had his little sister meddled in someone else's life beyond his own? Georgiana was proving to be a formidable matchmaker—the ladies of the ton would not stand a chance against her machinations.

"Come to dinner on Thursday," Darcy said suddenly. "You have not come to dine in some time."

"Very well." Bingley stood. "Was that all you wished to speak with me about? You have my forgiveness, you know. Everything has turned out for the best." He lowered his voice. "It is a sight more pleasurable to court away from Mrs. Bennet," he chuckled. "She is a dear woman, but likes to monopolize the conversation."

Darcy could do nothing but agree. Mrs. Bennet's interest in everything and everyone was difficult to stomach. It was one of his objections to Elizabeth's family. Such a loud gossip the lady was, always directing things as she liked them and looking down on anyone she disliked—just like Lady Catherine. His heart seized and his mind whirled as he continued to draw parallels between his aunt and Mrs. Bennet. What was the difference, really? Lady Catherine hunted gentlemen—*one* gentleman, that is—for her daughter, and Mrs. Bennet did the same for hers. His aunt had only her position to protect her from scorn. Being the daughter of an earl could shield a lady from much disparagement.

He felt even more guilty at this realization. How could he excuse the behavior of a relation and condemn the same behavior in another? Was he truly such a hypocrite?

"Darcy!" Bingley cried. "Are you well? You look as though you have swallowed a lemon."

"I am well, Bingley." Darcy put his head in his hand. "Merely had an unpleasant thought." He paused and looked up. "Do you ever have moments of clarity where you know you have made a mistake, and it takes you by surprise?"

Bingley nodded and chuckled. "Yes, I have them often. Sometimes they are little nudges, and other times it is as if someone fired a cannon at me. That was what it was like as I read the anonymous letter."

Smirking, Bingley bid Darcy farewell again, promising to come to dinner on Thursday. Alone once more, Darcy examined more closely his behavior in Meryton.

Elizabeth might have forgiven the man from the letters. That man had changed. He had improved himself and, in doing so, won her regard. He was not that man—not yet. But by George, he would work as hard as he could to become him!

A half hour later, Georgiana found him staring out the window. It was time for tea, and she wished for him to join her.

"Did you send Bingley a letter, too?" he asked abruptly as she came into his line of sight.

Startled, she gaped before flushing dark red. "Yes," she said, tilting her chin up defiantly. "He deserved to know."

"You are correct," Darcy said, sighing as he stood. "I know you took precautions—he told me—but do you comprehend how disastrous it would have been if someone—*anyone*—learned you wrote to an unmarried man?"

She smiled slyly. "It would probably be as disastrous as an unmarried man writing to an unmarried lady who currently stays near Cheapside." With that, she whirled around and flounced away. Irritated that his sister had once again got the better of him and, wondering if Elizabeth's influence was the cause, Darcy followed her. He needed a fortifying cup of tea to survive the day.

January 1812
Gracechurch Street
Elizabeth

Elizabeth's pen hovered above the paper. For three days, she had contemplated her reply to Mr. Darcy's last letter and was still no closer to starting than she had been when it arrived. Their meeting at Hatchard's had awakened something new within her. Being in Mr. Darcy's presence had befuddled and entranced her. She recalled the smell of cedar and sandalwood as he stood near; could almost feel the heat of his body next to her, even though she was alone in her chambers.

She knew he left their next meeting in her hands. It felt like a great responsibility. It was as if he were saying, "You decide if you wish to see me again, Elizabeth. You decide when you are ready to move forward." The respect such a sentiment portrayed touched her deeply. Yet, she did not feel equal to seeing him in person again. Her feelings of admiration were very new, and the realization she loved him was newer still. How had it come to this? In December, she had been pleased to share her bitter dislike with everyone, especially as Mr. Wickham spread tales of misuse amongst the populace.

Recalling her poor behavior made her feel ill. Mr. Darcy deserved to know what she had done. She had not been honest in her feelings—not really. The depth of her dislike she had concealed. What would he say if he knew? Did she have the courage to tell him? She knew she must, and so Elizabeth picked up her quill, dipped it in ink, and began to write.

My Dearest Mr. Darcy,

Your letter brought me more pleasure than I can convey. It seems that each time I open your correspondence, I discover yet another reason to be charmed by your words. How kind you are to express such regard for my musings on Miss Darcy's music. It would indeed be a great honor to hear her play, though I am quite certain that no one could do her talent justice except herself. But the thought of sharing in the beauty of Pemberley's quiet and hearing her melodies fills me with a curiosity I can hardly contain.

Your words about Miss Darcy's pain were both comforting and moving. It is clear how deeply you care for her, and I find that your affection for her only makes me more eager to know you better. I wish, with all my heart, that her tender spirit may heal completely. To be surrounded by such love and care, I have no doubt that her heart will, in time, be restored to its former lightness. Should I ever have the honor of spending more time with her, I shall endeavor to be a friend to her in every sense, as I too am drawn to her quiet strength.

As for your kind reflection on my preference for the color green, I am flattered to know that it seems so fitting. There is something hopeful about it, I agree, and as you say, it reflects my love for the countryside. It was not meant as a slight to blue; I assure you—such a color evokes thoughts of peace and tranquility, qualities I hold in the highest regard.

I wonder, though, if perhaps we might, someday, share a moment where the two of us are surrounded by the very hues we so admire.

Your fondness for lemon tarts, I must say, has left me with the most delightful image of us sharing a simple meal together. I confess that, though I would never accuse you of being greedy, I suspect that your enjoyment of the larger portion would be an inevitable result of your admirable self-discipline, though I shall not be so proud as to insist on being the one to take the smaller portion. A treat shared between friends is truly the most pleasurable of indulgences, and I look forward to the day when we may enjoy such a moment.

I am charmed, Mr. Darcy, by your reflections on dogs and cats. There is much to be said for both, of course, but I must admit, I have always had a certain admiration for the loyalty and companionship of a dog. I find it most endearing that you, too, hold them in such regard. And yet, I can easily imagine that, with your keen eye, you would appreciate the delicate nature of a cat's affections as well. Perhaps it is the case, then, that both animals could provide us with something we each cherish. I am convinced, though, that both would be quite content in your company, should you choose to keep them.

The thought of meeting you in person again and so soon after our encounter at Hatchard's fills my heart with a warmth that I can hardly disguise. To see the very thoughts you express in your letters come to life in your eyes again is a privilege I hope to experience soon. I, too, have longed for such a meeting, and I hope that the opportunity will quickly come again, so that we might discover, in each other's presence, what new joys await us.

Before we can do so, I find I am in need of some answers to questions that continue to plague me. I must be perfectly frank with you, sir. I have not behaved honorably where you are concerned. My dislike extended far past what I wrote in the first letters. Indeed, I despised you quite thoroughly. As I am sure you have ascertained, those ill feelings were fed by tales from one of our mutual acquaintances.

Mr. Wickham was eager to tell me how spitefully you used him. As I have looked back on that conversation, I realized he must have mixed the truth with lies to inflame my temper. And how he spread those tales after you left the area, when he told me he could never condemn you out of respect for your father—those recollections have told me much of his character.

I was not shy about voicing my disdain for you to all my neighbors. I confess, your insult at the assembly hurt me deeply. Even before Wickham's poisonous tales were told, I harbored a deep disgust for your behavior. I know now my feelings were that of wounded vanity, and I tried to soothe the hurt by disparaging and judging your behavior.

I will end this letter by begging for your forgiveness. You are not who I thought you were all those months ago. Indeed, you have become a dear friend, a trusted confidant, and my hopes for the future rest securely in your hands. I cannot speak the words—not yet. It would be too painful to pen them here, only to learn you cannot forgive me.

Until that moment arrives, know that I hold your words dear, and that I look forward with eager anticipation to whatever comes next.

With the deepest respect, and the fondest regard,
Elizabeth Bennet

She sat back in her chair, reading and rereading the letter. It felt as though she had rocks in her stomach. *There is nothing for it,* she thought, sanding and sealing the letter. He deserved to know. But how materially her feelings had changed! They were quite the opposite of what they had been. Would he believe her? She dearly hoped so.

February 1812
Darcy House
Darcy

The bell rang, alerting Darcy to Bingley's arrival. He was late—a good half hour, if the clock's time was true. It was very unlike him. His friend was more apt to arrive early than make others wait upon his arrival.

The door to the parlor opened. Georgiana sat at the pianoforte. She had been invited to dine with the gentlemen. Her companion, Mrs. Annesley, was to join them, making the entire thing very proper. Her playing stopped suddenly, and Darcy turned away from her to the doorway. In swept Caroline Bingley, followed by the Hursts and Mr. Bingley.

His friend looked utterly distraught. He shrugged his shoulders and mouthed, "I will explain later," before turning to greet Georgiana. His sister had come out from behind the pianoforte, and her face was contorted oddly, as if she was trying to keep an unpleasant expression off her face.

"Mr. Darcy!" Miss Bingley cried, swooping in and curtseying prettily. "I am so pleased to be here tonight! When Charles told me you had invited us to dinner, I said, 'How very fortunate we are to have Mr. and Miss Darcy as friends.' Did I not say that, Louisa?"

"Indeed you did!" Mrs. Hurst came forward, tipping her head in agreement. "Thank you very much, sir, for having us." Hurst had wandered off to the side table that held the decanter and had poured himself a glass of port. He did no more than a grunt in greeting before plopping down on the settee and taking a deep drink from his glass.

"Dinner is served." Thankful for the announcement, Darcy reluctantly extended his arm to Mrs. Hurst, the highest ranking lady in the room besides Georgiana. Miss Bingley stared daggers at her sister but latched onto his other arm, leaving Bingley to escort Georgiana and Mr. Hurst to escort Mrs. Annesley.

His unwanted guests chattered in his ear as he escorted them to their seats. His staff, ever efficient, had placed three extra settings at the table. Darcy deposited the sisters at the far end before moving to his spot at the head of the table. Miss Bingley looked irritated but said nothing. Georgiana sat on Darcy's right, in her usual spot, when they dined together. Hurst, Mrs. Annesley, and Bingley filled the other chairs. The table was terribly mismatched, but he found he did not care.

Darcy had looked forward to being able to converse freely with Bingley. He intended to tell his friend that he hoped they would one day be brothers by marriage. Despite the letter from Elizabeth which had arrived earlier that day, he still had hope for the future. Her words had cut him to the core, but it spoke well of her intelligence and character that she could admit she had been in error, and detect Wickham's lies without being explicitly informed of his poor behavior.

The letter sat on his desk. He had not responded to it, though he already knew he would offer Elizabeth his whole-hearted forgiveness. He would have plenty of time to brood now—conversation was always thin on the ground when the Bingley sisters were present.

"How is your playing, dear Georgiana?" Miss Bingley simpered. "It has been some time since I had the pleasure of hearing you play. Will you perform for us tonight? And how very fortunate you are in your brother! Attending a formal dinner at such a tender age—he must have great faith in you."

It was hardly a formal dinner at all. There was no proper seating, and there were only three courses planned. Miss Bingley's attempts to ingratiate herself with Georgiana were destined to fail. His sister edged away, responding only in monosyllables. Gone was the impertinent miss who had been present these past weeks, and in her place was a sullen, silent young lady.

The ladies departed immediately following the third course. Bingley let out a whoosh of breath and immediately began apologizing. "They were in the carriage before I knew what was happening!" he cried. "I went upstairs to dress for dinner, and Caroline asked where I was going, and like an idiot, I told her. Darcy, I am very sorry! I should have thrown them out when they got in."

"What is that?" spluttered Hurst. "We were not invited?" He looked at Darcy through blurry eyes. "Louisa never tells me about our dinner arrangements in advance—I had no cause to doubt her!" Turning to Darcy, he, too, expressed his apologies and begged forgiveness. "Deplorably rude," he muttered. "I shall have a talk with her as soon as we get home."

"Yes," agreed Bingley. "We will both confront them when we return to the house."

Darcy waved at them dismissively. "It is over and done," he said. "We must rescue Georgiana before they become too unbearable." He did not seem to be able to control his words—insulting the ladies to their relations! Yet, Bingley and Hurst laughed, standing to accompany him to the parlor where the ladies waited.

"Mr. Darcy!" Miss Bingley called, waving from her seat on the settee. "Come join me, sir!"

Darcy had no intention of putting himself in her grasp. He went instead and poured himself a glass of port. His attempt at avoiding her was short-lived, for she came to his side immediately.

"Charles has been out every day the past week," she hissed. "I do not know where he is going. Could he have learned of Miss Bennet's presence in town?"

"Your brother's business is his own. If he has and has decided to pursue her, then it is out of our hands." He took a swallow from his glass and moved a little further away.

"How can you speak so indifferently?" she whispered frantically. "Marriage to a country nobody will ruin him!" She ran a hand up his coat sleeve. "It will certainly prevent other more desirable events from occurring."

He turned and looked at her, hoping his gaze was as flat and cold as he intended. "I do not know what you mean," he said curtly.

Her hand climbed higher and rested on his chest. She was practically in his arms. Shifting away again so there was space between them, he cleared his throat.

"Do not be coy, sir," she purred. "It would be a perfect match—your sister and my brother...and then, when you are ready, perhaps you and I..." she trailed off, looking up at him expectantly. "Brothers at last—exactly what you and Charles have always wanted."

The irony was not lost on him. He and Bingley would be brothers, but not in the way Miss Bingley expected. "Let me be rightly understood," he said evenly, keeping his voice soft so as not to call attention to their conversation. "These matches to which you aspire will never take place."

She looked surprised. "Why not?" she asked. She sounded completely bemused. "My brother is practically a gentleman—she is a gentleman's daughter."

"An accident of birth has nothing to do with it." He stepped further away. "I will not encourage Georgiana to marry where there is no affection and I plan to set the example myself when I take a wife."

"But then all is well!" she cried, her voice pitching up a little. She sounded frantic. "I love you—I do! And I know you love me. We are of one accord in every decision. It is as if we were designed for each other!"

"Madam, you are utterly incorrect regarding my opinions." Bowing curtly, Darcy moved away, seating himself between Georgiana and Mrs. Annesley for the rest of the evening. It came as no surprise when Miss Bingley claimed a headache a short time later. The entire party left. Bingley promised to call the next day, and Darcy bid him farewell.

At sixes and sevens about his ruined evening, he sat down to compose his reply to Elizabeth's letter. Words came easier now, and the occupation soothed his mind. When he finished, he sanded and sealed it before retiring. It had been a long day.

February 1812
Gracechurch Street
Elizabeth

My Dearest Miss Elizabeth,

    Your letter fills me with more gratitude than I can express. To know that my words have touched you as they have, and that the very idea of hearing Georgiana's music brings you pleasure, gives me hope that our future conversations will continue to be filled with such warmth and understanding. I must confess that I, too, long for the day when you might hear her play in person—there is something in the very atmosphere of Pemberley that seems to invite such quiet, joyful moments. Perhaps you will meet her soon.

    Your compassion for Georgiana's struggles, and your kind words of comfort, move me beyond measure. To see the gentle and capable woman that you are, offering solace to my sister even in your letters, fills my heart with a sense of peace I did not expect to find. I have no doubt that Georgiana, with the support of a friend such as you, will indeed find her way back to the confidence and joy that are so truly her own. To know *that you are as eager to meet her as I am to see you both in each other's company brings a sense of promise for the future.*

I have pondered your reflection on the color green, and how it now reminds you of me, and I confess, it struck me deeply. How lucky I am to have found in you someone whose heart and spirit mirror the very qualities I admire most in the world. The idea of sharing a moment with you amidst these colors we so cherish fills me with anticipation. I imagine no company could be more perfect, no scenery more fitting.

As for the delightful tarts—ah, my dear friend, I am pleased to know you would not resist indulging in a larger portion! I confess, the temptation of a second helping would be difficult to resist, especially in the company of someone who knows the pleasure of such simple joys. I look forward to the day when we may share not only this treat, but perhaps many others in each other's company.

Your remarks about dogs and cats made me smile, for I, too, find the loyalty of a dog to be a rare and wonderful thing. Yet, as you say, the quiet, sometimes aloof affection of a cat holds its own charm. Perhaps we will find in each other's company an appreciation for both—though I dare say I would feel more inclined to adopt the more dependable of the two. I would be curious to hear more of your own thoughts on these creatures, and whether you would favor a dog's devotion or a cat's independence should you ever choose a companion of your own. Forgive me if I seem to be rambling or repeating myself—my thoughts are disjointed this evening.

Your mention of our meeting at Hatchard's brings a warmth to my chest that I can hardly contain. To see you again, to have the privilege of conversing with you face-to-face, is something I long for more than I can express. I hope, with all my heart, that such a meeting will soon take place, for there are so many things I would wish to share with you, and I find myself eager to learn from you as I have in these letters.

But, dear Miss Elizabeth, I must address the matter you have raised with such honesty and courage. It seems that, in your thoughts, you have carried a great burden—one that I can only hope has weighed less heavily upon you with the writing of this letter. I must assure you that I hold no anger towards you, nor any lingering resentment. What you have shared with me is not only moving, but speaks to a heart full of integrity. To know that you have reflected on past wrongs and sought to right them fills me with a respect I can scarcely put into words.

It is true that Mr. Wickham's account of our past was both injurious and misleading, and I can understand how it would have shaped your opinion of me. Do not berate yourself any longer. Mr. Wickham has deceived others with more years and wisdom to their name than you or I possess. As I have said before, my past is far from perfect, but I have never intentionally caused harm to anyone. I regret deeply that your opinion of me was so formed by deceit, and I can only be grateful that you have seen through it, for it has allowed us to arrive at this new understanding between us.

As for your apology, there is no need for it. We are all imperfect beings, and what I now value above all else is your honesty and the courage you have shown in writing these words to me. I have never considered you my enemy, and I confess that, as time has passed, I have come to think of you with the deepest and most ardent love.

What you write of your feelings for me is the most precious gift, and I shall cherish it always. However, I would not have you burden your heart with words that might not yet be ready to be spoken. All I ask is that you trust in time, and in the strength of our growing friendship, and know that whatever the future holds, I am honored to call you a friend, a confidante, and, in time, I hope, something even more.

Until that moment, know that I remain devotedly yours, with the greatest respect and the most profound affection.

Fitzwilliam Darcy

Mr. Darcy's letter arrived early that morning, put into her hands by Sally, who had by now become very interested to know who penned the mysterious letters. She did not ask Elizabeth directly, but the curiosity in her gaze could not be missed. Elizabeth could not satisfy it, however, and felt grateful the maid did nothing to prevent the correspondence.

The letter filled her with pleasure. How happy she felt he could forgive her so readily! She had hardly forgiven herself and still castigated herself each night as she lay next to a sleeping Jane.

She longed to see him, yet something still held her back. The man on paper was romantic, kind, and the embodiment of a man of character. She was unworthy of him. But had he not said they were both flawed? Imperfect beings? Dare she hope his words were the truth, that he admired her for her honesty and friendship?

Each day that passed made Elizabeth feel with more certainty she could not live without him. She looked into her future, and he was there. Her imagination conjured images of them picnicking in a field of flowers, him standing beside her as she played the pianoforte, turning the pages as she sang along to the music. Every situation she could think of played in her head, tantalizing her with the possibilities.

Aunt Gardiner interrupted her thoughts, bidding Elizabeth to prepare for their trip to Bond Street. Their new gowns were ready for a final fitting. Elizabeth tucked the letter into her hiding spot. The green velvet bulged, and she reminded herself to move the missives when she returned.

Jane awaited her in the vestibule, her outerwear donned. "Mr. Bingley is to join us for ices," she confided. "He will meet us at Madame Dubois' in an hour."

"Ices in February?" Elizabeth cried. "It is already far too cold outside."

"You may have hot chocolate if you prefer." Jane stuck her tongue out playfully and winked. "There is something thrilling about eating a cold dessert in the winter."

"You may think that if it gives you comfort," Elizabeth groaned. "I shall indeed have hot chocolate! Nothing could tempt me to eat a frozen treat when it is frosty outside."

Madame Dubois had their order ready when they arrived. Elizabeth had never had a fitting finished so quickly. Her new gowns, one blue, one cream, and the last a beautiful blush color, were exquisite. She fingered the last one, picturing herself wearing it when she met Darcy again. *But perhaps the blue...* her gaze drifted to the garment made in his favorite color. Shaking her head at her nonsensical, sentimental thoughts, she thanked Madame Dubois. An assistant stepped forward and whisked the gowns away to package them.

Jane went next, and before another half hour was gone, they were finished. Aunt Gardiner sent Jones to the carriage with their parcels and they meandered towards Gunter's. The brisk wind bit their cheeks, but they laughed, linking arms and stopping occasionally to point at a window display. When at last they arrived at Gunter's, they were more than ready to be inside and out of the wind.

February 1812
Gracechurch Street
Elizabeth

Elizabeth read Mr. Darcy's letter again. She traced his signature and pictured his face in her mind. She loved him—of that she had no doubt. How it was possible for her feelings to undergo such a change and in so short a time, she did not know. Every ill feeling was now resolved, and he had forgiven her for her hasty judgments of the past.

Why, then, do I hesitate to arrange our meeting? she thought. *What holds me back?* Was it because she struggled to imagine herself as his wife? No, that was not it. She had pictured their future together many times. *Maybe it is because my mind cannot reconcile the man in the letters with the man from Hertfordshire.* But he had changed—he wrote of it.

It had been two days since she received this missive, and she did not wish to delay replying any longer. Settling at the little table where her writing box stood, she pulled a piece of paper towards her and began to write.

Dearest Mr. Darcy,

I find myself once again reflecting on our last meeting at Hatchard's, and I cannot help but feel a great sense of longing for the conversation we were denied. Though our exchange was but a brief one, my thoughts return to it over and over, as if there is a certain weight or significance to the words we shared that I did not fully comprehend at the time. How often I wish I had not been obliged to take my leave so hastily—perhaps it would have allowed me the time and courage to speak more freely, to unburden myself of thoughts I have not yet found the courage to express. I often wonder what more we might have shared, and how my own thoughts might have been clarified had we continued our discourse. But, alas, such musings are idle now, and I am left only with the wish that I had more boldly seized the opportunity for a longer conversation.

Your forgiveness, sir, is something I hold in the highest regard, and I am endlessly grateful for it. The very thought that you might have dismissed me entirely due to my previous behavior was a fear I carried with me for some time, and I am truly relieved to know that such a fate was not mine. Your words, so kind and understanding, fill me with a profound sense of peace. I did, indeed, fear that I had lost your good opinion forever, and to know that it remains is a gift of which I shall never cease to be thankful. It is a great comfort to me that my actions, though misguided, have not caused irreparable harm to our relationship. I treasure your continued regard with all my heart.

That said, there remains a matter that troubles me, one that I must raise with you—Mr. Wickham. As you well know, he is a man whose charm has won him the favor of many, especially amongst the ladies. I cannot deny that his manner is most disarming, and I am aware of how easily he could be mistaken for a man of virtue. But I now find myself questioning whether I can, in good conscience, allow him to remain within the circle of my friends and family, especially if all you have told me is true. I trust you implicitly, Mr. Darcy, and I do not doubt the accuracy of your report. But I wonder, given the man's past and the deceit he has so skillfully woven, whether it is safe to allow him to continue to move freely amongst those I care for.

It is troubling to consider that he, a man without fortune and with little to recommend him aside from his charm, might still find a way to ensnare the affections of some unsuspecting young woman. Can I, in good conscience, allow him to behave as a gentleman in the presence of my friends? His history, as you have shared it, suggests he is more than capable of using his wit and his charm to mislead others, and I fear that his actions in the past may not be confined to those early indiscretions. The thought that he might repeat such behavior, or worse, lead others into similar ruin, weighs heavily upon me.

Yet, I find myself in a most difficult position, for though I know what I must do, the information I hold is not mine alone to share. Mr. Wickham's actions, and the impact of those actions, are his own, and yet I cannot help but feel responsible for the welfare of those around me. I am caught between the desire to protect those I love and the knowledge that I cannot act alone in this matter. I cannot speak to my father about it—though we have always been open with one another, I fear he would dismiss the matter entirely. His indifference to the more serious aspects of life, particularly those involving the welfare of my sisters, leaves me with little hope that he would take my concerns seriously. Perhaps it is my own naiveté, but I cannot help but believe that there are men who require no fortune to ruin a young lady. And Mr. Wickham, with his charm and his ability to deceive, is surely one such man.

I am at a loss as to how to proceed, Mr. Darcy. I know that the right course of action must be taken, but I fear the consequences of making the wrong choice. Your advice would be invaluable to me, and I eagerly await your thoughts on how best to navigate this troubling situation.

But I must confess, I cannot end this letter on such a bleak note, for I wish to share with you a more amusing account from my recent adventures. The other day, Jane and I made our way to Bond Street, where I indulged in a most unexpected delight. As I sipped my hot chocolate, Jane, ever playful, added some of her vanilla ice to my beverage. Initially, I must admit, I was rather put out—the cold ice did little to enhance the warmth of the drink, and I found the combination somewhat vexing. But to my surprise, the flavors melded together far better than I could have imagined, and I must say, I was quite taken with the result! In fact, I am now quite determined to try this again the next time I visit Gunter's—hot chocolate with a scoop of vanilla ice on top. I wonder what you might think of such a combination?

I do hope this letter finds you in good spirits, Mr. Darcy, and that your day has been as pleasant as mine has been, despite my earlier concerns. I look forward to your response with great eagerness and anticipation.

Yours most sincerely,
Elizabeth Bennet

She sanded and sealed the missive, determined it would be in Mr. Darcy's hand before the day ended.

February 1812
Darcy House
Darcy

The receipt of Elizabeth's letter was the highlight of the evening. Darcy had waited anxiously for word from her for two days and wondered what could have delayed her reply. At long last, he held her letter in his hand. Without delay, he went to his study and broke the seal, unfolding the paper to see what she had written.

The beginning contained serious matters, and he frowned as he contemplated her conundrum. Richard had said similar things after Georgiana's fiasco last summer. "You have let that blackguard run amok long enough," his cousin had growled. "How long before your inaction allows Wickham to ruin another?" And here in his hand were similar concerns, penned by the woman he loved.

Wickham has had more than enough time to remedy his behavior, he thought. *Have I promoted his behavior unintentionally by doing nothing to curb his excesses?* Darcy had realized long ago that his father's largesse had likely contributed to Wickham's sense of entitlement. He had been raised as a second son and believed all the rights and privileges of that position were his. And neither the old Mr. Darcy nor his son had ever done anything to show the man otherwise.

A firm resolve came over him. He penned a quick note to his cousin, Colonel Richard Fitzwilliam, asking him to call upon Darcy House whenever he could, and sent it with a footman. Within a half hour, his cousin appeared.

"I thought it would be faster to come than to send a note suggesting another time," he said cheerfully. "What did you wish to discuss?"

"Wickham," Darcy said shortly, watching as Richard's cheerful countenance turned to a scowl.

"Has he come begging again?" he spat angrily. "I warn you, if I ever see him again, I shall—"

"He is in Hertfordshire," Darcy cut in. "We encountered each other last autumn whilst I stayed with Bingley. The miscreant has joined the local militia, if you can believe it." Here, he paused, fixing a serious stare on his cousin's face. "I believe he may be a threat to the local populace," Darcy continued. "There are many innocent women there, and you and I both know he has likely run up debts with every merchant in town."

Richard leaned forward, a sly smile spreading across his face. "What has this to do with me?" he asked, though Darcy felt certain his cousin knew exactly what Darcy wanted.

Drawing in a breath, he came around the side of his desk. "I have come to the conclusion that it is time to stop protecting him," he murmured. "My father would be ashamed of the man his godson has become, and I dishonor his memory by continuing to humor his excesses."

Richard clapped his hands and stood up. "Well done, man! Tell me, what has prompted this change of heart?" His expression grew concerned. "Is Georgie well?" he asked.

"My sister has nothing to do with it," Darcy replied. He could feel his cheeks growing red. The last thing he needed was Richard prying into his affairs.

His cousin's expression now looked like the cat got the cream. "Oh, ho!" he cried. "It is a *girl*, is it not? What else would move a man to such a gesture? Even your sister's near calamity could not sway you to my way of thinking!"

Darcy shook his head, thinking it was better not to answer, but Richard would have none of it.

"Do not attempt to deny it," he chortled. "Does Mama know yet? Or better yet, Lady Catherine! Have you declined to share this news with our most *interested* relation?"

"You are not to say a word," Darcy growled. "Any misstep could cost me the lady's heart."

Richard guffawed and went to the table where the decanter stood. "What lady would refuse *you?*" he asked, pouring himself some of the amber liquid.

"She would." Darcy sounded so certain that it caused his cousin to look up in shock. "She refused her father's heir," he continued, ignoring the incredulous expression. He went to the table and took the decanter from the dumbfounded Richard and set it back down.

His cousin whistled. "You have found a rare treasure," he said appreciatively. "May we all be so blessed with a woman who sees beyond fortune." He downed the glass in one gulp and set it with a loud thunk on the tray. "Now, what will you have me do? You hold enough markers to see him in debtor's prison."

"I leave it up to you," Darcy said. "I do not know if I could resist aiding him if I knew his fate."

Richard grinned malevolently and nodded. "Do you have the markers here?" he asked. "Or must you send to Pemberley?"

"As fortune would have it, they are here." Darcy went to his wall safe and twirled the dial to open it. He extracted a stack of markers, tied together with twine, and passed them to his cousin. Richard pocketed them immediately, and Darcy wondered if the colonel thought he would change his mind.

"Very good, then." Richard moved towards the door. "I shall see to it directly. And I expect to be introduced to the paragon who has captured your heart at the earliest possible opportunity." And then he was gone.

Darcy sank into the nearby armchair and put his head in his hands. The guilt invoked by Elizabeth's letter had been a powerful motivator. It forced him to look at his decisions—where they concerned Mr. Wickham. Always, he had acted in a way which offered the least resistance or trouble to himself. It was not the best way to manage affairs. He could not call himself worthy of a good woman if he could not make difficult decisions.

Removing Wickham from the world would prevent further heartache. He left a string of ruined women, broken hearts, and mounting debts in his path. Whilst Wickham's decisions were his own, Darcy's lack of action condemned him. Well, it would not be that way any longer. He would remedy the situation, protecting Elizabeth's family, the citizens of Meryton, and the merchants in the area all at once. He could do no less and still call himself a gentleman.

February 1812
Gracechurch Street
Elizabeth

Mr. Bingley arrived, his expression detailing his frustration to the ladies gathered in Aunt Gardiner's parlor. "Caroline attempted to waylay me again," he groused. "Ever since learning I have been calling upon you, she hovers needlessly, asking me to escort her here and there on a whim to prevent my going out alone. Her actions do nothing to further her aims and only seek to frustrate me."

Jane patted his hand sympathetically but offered no solution. They were not yet engaged, though Elizabeth thought it would be any day now. When they were, her sister would voice her opinions more readily. Last night, as they lay in bed, Jane had whispered her thoughts to her dearest sister.

"I will not have Caroline in my house," she said earnestly. "It is clear she holds me in no regard, and I will not be made to feel a stranger in my own home."

"Brava, Jane," Elizabeth whispered back. "She will usurp your rights as mistress—you know she will. But you must speak to Bingley about it. Will he have the fortitude to refuse his sister a home?"

Jane had not answered. When she made no reply, Elizabeth encouraged her to ponder the situation before accepting a proposal.

"She has become unbearable!" Bingley continued, throwing his hands in the air. "I cannot abide her any longer. Though I have been staying with the Hursts until now, I am searching for another town house to purchase. I shall remove myself from Caroline's presence as soon as may be—and she will *never* be welcome in my home as anything but a guest again!"

It seemed Jane would have no need for that discussion with her beloved. Miss Bingley's machinations had backfired. Instead of convincing her brother to abandon Jane, she had pushed him more fully into the 'unacceptable lady's' arms. Elizabeth smirked, watching Mr. Bingley sit very close to Jane. He offered her a single hothouse flower, likely purchased from a street side vendor on his way to Gracechurch Street. Jane blushed prettily and took the bloom, pressing it to her nose and inhaling the scent.

Aunt Gardiner caught Elizabeth's eye and nodded. She stood. "I must go see to something with Cook," she said. "Elizabeth, will you accompany me?"

It sounded very much like something Mama would say, but Elizabeth agreed without complaint. Perhaps a few minutes alone would be all Mr. Bingley needed to propose to Jane.

Elizabeth almost collided with Sally in the hall, who offered her a missive and an apology as she stumbled a little.

"Thank you," Elizabeth said, taking the letter from the maid. "Do you mind if I go upstairs and read this, Aunt?" she asked.

"Charlotte Collins is a diligent correspondent," Mrs. Gardiner said, raising an eyebrow. Skepticism written on her face, she nodded her agreement and continued to the kitchens.

I shall have to tell her everything soon, Elizabeth thought as she climbed the stairs. There was too much evidence that the person she exchanged letters with was nearby. Her aunt was not unintelligent and had likely deduced that much already. How long her curiosity would be kept at bay remained to be seen.

She broke the seal almost as soon as she had closed the door, going to the bed and sitting upon it. The familiar scrawl comforted her, and she began to read.

Dearest Miss Elizabeth,

Your letter reached me at a most opportune moment, and I find myself thoroughly engaged by the reflections you so graciously shared. It is with both warmth and a certain sense of regret that I now think of our brief meeting at Hatchard's. Had I known how much you would cherish our conversation, I would have done all in my power to extend it, to allow us both the space to speak more freely and without interruption. I, too, find myself remembering that moment, and wonder what words we might have exchanged had we both been afforded a little more time. I look forward to the day when I might be able to converse with you at length, without the constraints that the world too often places upon us.

As for your kind words of gratitude, I must assure you, madam, that my good opinion of you is unwavering. If anything, the humility and honesty with which you have written strengthens it. Your sincerity is one of the many qualities that has made me so grateful to count you as a correspondent, and, in time, I hope—though I must be patient and take nothing for granted—that our friendship may continue to deepen and flourish. The gift of your continued regard is one I will treasure always, and I thank you again for your openness and for the kindness you have shown me in your words.

Your concerns regarding Mr. Wickham, however, trouble me greatly. I understand the weight of your thoughts, and I share your unease. The man's charm, as you say, is most disarming, and for too long, I have dismissed concerns that his presence in circles such as ours may lead others astray. My cousin is amongst the most vocal in this regard. He holds a deep dislike for Wickham and has pressured me for many years to do something about the miscreant. The matter is not one to be taken lightly, for as you rightly note, Mr. Wickham's ability to deceive, though it may have served him well in the past, is not a trait to be trusted. His conduct in the past has been, as I have shared with you, less than honorable, and I agree with you completely that such behavior cannot be permitted to continue unbridled. I now have only to castigate myself for allowing him to go unchecked for so long.

It is clear that you have no desire to cause scandal, yet you find yourself in a position where silence might lead to greater harm. Your fear of speaking out is understandable, given the reluctance of your father to engage with such matters seriously, and I fully comprehend your hesitation to burden others with information that could bring undue distress.

I have been caught in a difficult place—bound by the need to protect those I care for, but constrained by the memory of the boy who was my friend—who my father loved as another son. Upon reflection, I believe it to be my duty to share my knowledge. It is the honorable way forward.

Should you find yourself with other concerns, know that I am more than happy to assist in whatever way I can. Should you need me to speak further on the matter or to lend my support in any way, I am at your service. I would never wish for you to feel alone in this, *Miss Elizabeth*, and together we might find the best way onward.

After such heavy musings, I must confess that I found your anecdote about the hot chocolate most delightful, and I am pleased that such a small experiment turned out to be such a success. I must admit, I had my doubts when I first read of your drink being altered with vanilla ice, but your reported result is truly unexpected! I shall have to try it myself at Gunter's next time Georgiana persuades me to take her there. Pleasure can be found in the most unlikely of places, and I find a certain charm in these small indulgences. I daresay that a cup of hot chocolate enhanced with vanilla ice might make for a most agreeable treat. When the opportunity presents itself, I hope we may share in such a pleasure together.

I look forward with eager anticipation to our next meeting—whether by letter or in person—and I remain, as always, devotedly yours.

With the greatest respect and warmest regards,
Fitzwilliam Darcy

His words comforted Elizabeth, though she wondered what this 'way forward' meant. *Is he to ride to Hertfordshire and proclaim Mr. Wickham's sins? I do hope not—he would not be well received!* Panicked, she went to the writing table and readied a piece of paper. All thoughts of Jane and an imminent proposal fled her thoughts. Mr. Darcy needed a reply post-haste.

February 1812
Darcy House
Darcy

Nothing could have surprised Darcy more than receiving a reply to Elizabeth's letter the very day he sent one to her. There was usually a day or so between her missives—he tried to be patient, but rarely succeeded. Georgiana, content that her brother could manage his own romance, did no more than ask about Elizabeth once in a while. She was impatient to meet the lady officially, and had sketched a passable likeness as a gift to her brother. The eyes were not exactly right—maybe they were too fine to be captured on canvas.

Without another thought, he broke the seal and began to read.

Dearest Fitzwilliam,

I write to you again, not merely to respond to your previous letter, but because I feel it necessary to offer a word of caution regarding the matter of Mr. Wickham, as it weighs heavily on my mind. While I am confident in your good intentions and the sincerity with which you seek to rectify this wrong, I feel compelled to warn you, with the utmost respect and care, that the manner in which you approach this situation may not be as straightforward as you might hope.

As you are aware, I have no great love for Mr. Wickham, though I championed him so thoroughly last autumn. His charms have deceived many, and his words acted to further poison me against you. I certainly made no effort to hide my disdain from my neighbors. I fear they would recall my dislike if I were not present to counter it, and would work to prevent you from succeeding.

Indeed, the town of Meryton, as I am sure you are aware, has been more than receptive to his tales of supposed mistreatment at your hands. They have embraced his version of events, and in those circles, he is seen as a martyr, wronged by 'the likes of you.' The stories he has spread, true or false, have taken root in the minds of the good people there, and it would be no exaggeration to say that they would be inclined to believe his account over yours, given the widespread sympathy he enjoys.

Therefore, I must caution you against rushing forth with the entire truth, however justified it may be. Should you go to Meryton and attempt to correct the narrative with your own account, I fear you will not only find yourself met with disbelief, but you will be mocked, scorned, and possibly even laughed out of the village. The power of Mr. Wickham's charm and the ease with which he has twisted his story has given him an almost unassailable position in the eyes of many.

I say this not to discourage you, but to ensure that you approach this delicate matter with caution. If your intentions are to expose Mr. Wickham's deceit, I would advise you to consider the consequences carefully, for the path you wish to take may not yield the results you expect. Should you decide to confront him directly, you must be prepared for the potential backlash from the very people who have believed in his version of events. And should you take this public matter to those who have the *power to act on it, you must be prepared to face skepticism, if not outright ridicule, from the town.*

As much as I wish for the truth to be known, I fear that the present circumstances may not allow for a straightforward resolution. I know you wish to act with honor, and I fully support that, but I cannot ignore the practical implications of what such a course of action might entail. Therefore, I implore you to weigh carefully the consequences of any action you take, and to proceed with caution, keeping in mind that Meryton is not a place where truth always prevails over charm.

I trust in your judgment, Fitzwilliam, and I know that whatever course you choose, you will do so with the utmost integrity. But I must beg you to be mindful of the risks and to ensure that you are prepared for the reaction you might receive. I write this not to dissuade you from action, but to remind you of the realities of the situation at hand.

I look forward to your thoughts on this matter and await your next letter with great anticipation.

Yours most sincerely,
Elizabeth Bennet

Seeing her use his given name sent a thrill through him. She had not done so yet, and he had abstained, waiting for her to be ready for such familiarity. Never had he dreamed it would occur before they met in person again. Oh, how he had longed to whisper her name in her ear. He would kiss her hand and proclaim how ardently he admired and loved her.

Shaking himself from his imaginings, he reread her letter a little slower. Her concern warmed his heart. She had no need to fear, however. He had already taken such information into account. It was why he had sent Richard in his place. As a colonel in the regulars, he had more sway with the local militia colonel. His presence was commanding, too. As an added benefit, Wickham feared Darcy's cousin more than any other.

Wishing to ease Elizabeth's fears, he penned another letter, wondering if it would be too obvious if he sent it immediately. She had not mentioned any suspicions about the missives—were there any? He supposed he ought to ask and resolved to add it to his letter. A wicked part of him hoped to be discovered. He would welcome any excuse to marry her as quickly as possible. It would be better if she were ready, however, and so he tucked those musings away in the back of his head, determined to see this strange courtship to its natural conclusion as soon as Elizabeth felt ready.

Nodding as if to confirm this new resolve, he moved from his comfortable armchair to his desk. Uncapping the ink bottle, he dipped his newly mended pen into the black liquid and began to compose a new letter.

February 1812
Gracechurch Street
Elizabeth

*D*earest Elizabeth,

    I received your letter with both gratitude and a measure of regret. Your caution and wisdom, as always, have been most valuable, and I see clearly the predicament in which I would find myself should I pursue this matter in the manner I initially intended. You are entirely right that the circumstances of Meryton and Mr. Wickham's hold over the town would likely thwart any attempt to restore my name there.

    However, I must inform you I have taken a different course of action, one that, I hope, will achieve a more satisfactory resolution without subjecting either of us to the public scorn you so rightly fear. In lieu of traveling to Meryton myself, I have entrusted the matter to my cousin, Colonel Fitzwilliam. He is a man of both discretion and force when necessary, and his presence in the village will, I believe, be met with far less resistance than mine would have. His long-standing connections within the military and his own status in the community will afford him the necessary respect to be taken seriously, where I, as you have so wisely warned, might have been met with ridicule.

Colonel Fitzwilliam has likely already arrived in Meryton and is, as I write, making arrangements to address Mr. Wickham's debts. As you know, Mr. Wickham has long been a man of poor fiscal habits, and it seems his debts, once easily ignored by those around him, can no longer be overlooked. My cousin has in his possession the appropriate markers and notes that confirm Wickham's financial obligations, and he will call in these debts in full. Should Mr. Wickham fail to settle them, Colonel Fitzwilliam will ensure that he faces the consequences befitting such neglect.

It is my belief that once the weight of these debts becomes clear to Mr. Wickham, he will be forced to confront the realities of his situation, and perhaps, if the good people of Meryton see his true character exposed in such a way, they may reconsider their favorable view of him. Whether this will be enough to dislodge him from the good opinion of the townsfolk, I cannot say—but it will certainly be a start.

As for you, my dear Elizabeth, I assure you that your part in this matter will remain a quiet one. You have spoken out of your concerns with great care and clarity, but I shall make every effort to protect you from any fallout that may arise from these actions. You need not worry yourself over how this may be received in the village or fear that your reputation might be tarnished by your association with me in this matter.

I will leave the rest to Colonel Fitzwilliam's capable hands, trusting that he will deal with Mr. Wickham in a manner that reflects both his duty and his honor, without stirring unnecessary scandal. Should any further difficulties arise from this course of action, I will be sure to keep you informed. But, for the moment, I am confident that this will resolve the matter without the need for me to expose myself to the public contempt you so wisely cautioned me about.

In the meantime, I look forward to your response, and I remain, as always, most sincerely yours.

Fitzwilliam Darcy

PostScript: I almost forgot—we shirk propriety further with every missive we exchange. Is there no suspicion, either from your relations or the servants? I do not wish to place you in any untenable circumstances.

She noted his use of her Christian name, and it filled her with delight. Vaguely, she recalled using *his* given name in her last—he had returned the sentiment in this letter. It thrilled her from the top of her head to the tips of her toes.

Elizabeth knew not how to answer. Of course, her aunt was suspicious. The arrival of yet another missive—*after* the post had arrived—had caused Aunt Gardiner to frown in her niece's direction. She could say nothing, however, for Mr. Bingley and Jane deserved the attention. He had proposed, and the eldest Miss Bennet had accepted with pleasure. She was of age, and so Mr. Bennet's consent was not needed; however, she wished for his blessing as soon as possible. Uncle Gardiner was prevailed upon to write a letter to his brother-in-law, and Mr. Bingley included a note within the missive, offering to pay for an express to take it to Longbourn immediately.

His offer was accepted. "You do realize that Mama will know about your engagement by the end of the day?" Elizabeth teased her sister. "She will write to you of lace and wedding clothes before tomorrow."

Jane was too happy to care. Aunt Gardiner offered to take her to purchase her wedding clothes, and a request for more funds was included in the letter to Mr. Bennet.

"Do not think you have escaped an interrogation, Lizzy," Mrs. Gardiner said in low tones. "I will have an explanation."

Elizabeth flushed red but did not make a reply. Mr. Darcy was an honorable man. There was no fear of a tarnished reputation—he would not allow it.

Mr. Bingley made ready to depart, citing a meeting with his solicitor that he had put off twice already. "I have more to discuss with him now, however," he continued jovially as he bid the ladies farewell. "Shall I accompany you to Bond Street tomorrow?"

It was agreed that he would arrive to take them thither after the midday meal the next day. Elizabeth managed to avoid the confrontation with her aunt until after supper. Whilst Jane and Uncle Gardiner read books quietly in the corner, Mrs. Gardiner came across the room and sat next to Elizabeth on the settee.

She leaned close and whispered in her niece's ear. "They are not from Mrs. Collins, are they?" she asked.

Elizabeth went red and shook her head. She offered no more and inwardly cringed at the speculative, disapproving look on her aunt's face.

"Keep your counsel, Elizabeth," she said, "for a little longer. Your reputation is nothing to play with. But I am a hopeless romantic, and so I shall give you until the day after February 14th to tell me everything."

St. Valentine's Day. Somehow, Elizabeth had not realized it was so close. *Perfect,* she thought. *It is a most excellent day to arrange a meeting.* And it was only five days away.

February 1812
Darcy House
Darcy

*D*earest Fitzwilliam,

    Your letter was, as always, both thoughtful and considerate, and I confess that I felt an overwhelming sense of relief upon reading of your new course of action. Colonel Fitzwilliam's presence in Meryton will no doubt smooth the path ahead, and I find myself far less anxious about the potential for ridicule or scandal. I am reassured by your good judgment and, as ever, impressed by your ability to find a solution that is both effective and elegant.

    And yet, I must admit, the idea of Mr. Wickham's debts catching up with him brings a certain sense of wicked pleasure. How thoroughly satisfying it must be to see him finally face the consequences of his actions! Though I confess, I do not delight in anyone's misfortune, I cannot help but feel a little satisfaction at the thought that his charm might no longer serve him so well. I am certain, however, that you and your cousin will handle the matter with great dignity—and perhaps with a dash of amusement at the irony of it all.

As for me, dear Fitzwilliam, I will take your assurances to heart and endeavor to remain quiet, as you so kindly suggest. It is a relief to know that I need not trouble myself with the negative consequences of our respective actions. I must admit, I find it a little difficult to imagine not having any part to play in such an exciting affair. I do so love a good intrigue, and I must confess that the idea of seeing Mr. Wickham finally unmasked gives me more enjoyment than it should.

But let us speak of lighter things, for I am sure you grow weary of hearing me dwell on Mr. Wickham and his debts. I do hope you will indulge me for a moment longer. Your PostScript caught my attention, and I must admit, it is a question I too have pondered. You ask if there is any suspicion from my relations or the servants, and I must tell you my aunt questioned me thoroughly tonight. She has given me a deadline of sorts before she will demand answers. The art of correspondence is an old one, and while we may be somewhat less than proper in our exchanges, our situation is all the better for it.

On occasion, I feel a certain… flutter in my chest when I open a letter from you, wondering if anyone might observe the sudden softness in my expression or the warm glow in my cheeks. It is a secret delight, one that I shall continue to savor. Now, my dear sir, I believe the time has come for us to arrange a meeting. Therefore, I beg your attendance at Hyde Park on February the 14th at two o'clock in the afternoon. I will secure the use of my uncle's carriage and wait for you near the fountain. A fair warning, sir, that I plan to cast aside all propriety and give you a full recital of my sentiments at that time. It is highly improper for me to be the first to do so, but I care not! I shall speak the words in my heart and do so without hearing yours first—unless, of course, you find it necessary to make your next missive an even more ardent declaration. I might not resist the temptation to answer in kind!

I eagerly await your next letter, Fitzwilliam, and am, as always, yours most sincerely.

Elizabeth

Darcy could not breathe. *She has named a date!* he thought excitedly. At long last, Elizabeth wished to meet him intentionally. And on St. Valentine's Day! He had never observed the holiday before—to do so would invite unwanted attachments.

Standing abruptly, he took the letter and rushed to the parlor in search of Georgiana. His sister stitched quietly in the corner. Mrs. Annesley dozed in a chair by the fire. It was enough privacy for them to speak in quiet whispers.

"I need your assistance," he said without preamble, sitting beside her. "Elizabeth wishes to meet on St. Valentine's Day."

Georgiana muffled a squeal and took his hand. "That is a very good sign!" she cried. "Oh, it is all working out exactly how I planned!"

"But what do I do?" Darcy spoke frantically. "It is four days distant—is there time for a romantic gesture? What is acceptable? Cards? Chocolate? I am not a proponent of offering empty promises I have no intention of keeping."

Georgiana patted his cheek. "Any promise you give her better be sincere," she warned. "Elizabeth is too intelligent to believe empty words. Will you propose?"

Darcy shrugged. "I want to—I love her dearly. But will she accept? Is she ready for me to speak my heart? Her letter claims she is, but I do not dare hope."

His sister giggled excitedly. "Let us review her letters," she said. "We will arrange an array of tokens that speak of your affections. And you must give me a list of all her attributes you admire."

Feeling slightly better about the situation, Darcy nodded. He and Georgiana spoke quietly, trading ideas and making arrangements to purchase tokens of his esteem. He felt everything was a tad meager. Darcy wanted to offer Elizabeth the world, not a delicate card or a bouquet. Whatever he presented to his love, he wanted it to speak of his ardent admiration. Each trinket, each token, must tell a story. Elizabeth must not be in any doubt of his affections by the time he had showered her with gifts.

She is not the sort to want material items, he mused. *But it would not hurt to have them, anyway.* He could demonstrate his love in a thousand ways if given the opportunity.

As he readied for bed, he remembered a particularly lovely brooch his mother had left him. It was intended for the next Mrs. Darcy, and would be perfect to give Elizabeth. Making a quick note so he would not forget to have it cleaned, he climbed into his bed and fell into an exhausted slumber.

February 1812
Bond Street
Elizabeth

Their excursion to Bond Street ended in a manner that had become tradition. Aunt Gardiner, Jane, and Elizabeth took their usual table, a larger one in the center of the shop with a view of the doorway. Mr. Bingley would join them soon after he finished business with his solicitor. Jane's gaze drifted to the door every few minutes, and Elizabeth smothered a laugh as her sister's foot tapped the ground impatiently. He arrived twenty minutes later, looking harried and irritated. "Caroline is out at the shops," he said. "She called my name, but I pretended I did not hear and took a less direct path. I rode my horse, and I believe I managed to get away from her."

The bell at the door rang, and Miss Bingley walked through the door.

"I am afraid not, sir," Aunt Gardiner said in low tones, nodding in that direction. Mr. Bingley turned around and groaned as he noted his sister. "Maybe she will not see me."

"Do not depend upon it," Elizabeth murmured. "She has already noted Jane." Only a blind man would miss Jane in a crowded room. The eldest Miss Bennet was lovely even after weeping.

Miss Bingley drew closer. Her hands were in a fur muff, and her fur-lined cloak billowed out behind her as she walked. "Charles!" she cried. "You told me you were off to your club."

"And so I will be, right after I have a vanilla ice." He shrugged. "Do you not have a shop to visit?"

Miss Bingley frowned. "No. I believe I shall join you. You would not mind giving up your seat, would you, Miss Eliza?" She batted her eyes, her gaze scornful as she looked the Bennet sisters up and down.

"I think not, Miss Bingley. There is room at the table. Pray, move a chair and join us." Elizabeth tried to be kind—for Jane's sake, but the lady irritated her.

She seemed to war with the indignity of picking up her own chair and moving it, and leaving the store altogether. If the first, she would lower herself in front of a tradesman. If the second, then her brother would be as good as alone with Miss Bennet. Elizabeth snickered under her breath. That seemed to spur Miss Bingley into action, and she picked up a chair. She sat next to her brother, moving her chair as far away from Aunt Gardiner as possible. Her eyes glinted with ill intent, and she turned her calculating gaze upon the Bennet sisters.

"How very...surprising...to see you all here. Together. Charles, when did you learn Miss Bennet was in town?" Her words were sickly sweet. "Mr. Darcy tried to keep you too busy to discover her presence."

The entire table went silent. Mr. Bingley looked furious, and Jane looked hurt. Elizabeth struggled to keep her expression neutral, even as her heart squeezed painfully. She had once suspected Mr. Darcy played a role in keeping Mr. Bingley in town, but after their letters, she had absolved him of the crime, believing him to be too romantic to destroy another's happiness in such a way.

"I do not know what you are babbling about, Caroline," Bingley said woodenly. He reached out and took Jane's hand. "If you wish to spit venom, please leave. Your vitriolic words should not spoil our afternoon."

Miss Bingley looked triumphant, no doubt pleased to have upset Jane. She stood regally, nodding her head at each member of the party before turning to leave.

"If she meant to infuriate me, she succeeded," Mr. Bingley said sullenly. "Now, shall we order ices?"

"Does she know you proposed yet?" Aunt Gardiner asked slyly.

"No. And I have no intention of informing her until *after* the wedding." Mr. Bingley scooped up Jane's hand and kissed it. "She will not be able to interfere then."

The other ladies chuckled, but Elizabeth said nothing. She drank her hot chocolate without tasting a thing. The betrayal stung, and her mind tried to reason through everything. Too numb to process any thoughts, she resolved to think on the matter later. Maybe then it would all make sense.

In the past, her usual response would be to act immediately. She longed to pen a letter to Mr. Darcy, spewing vitriol and accusations. Her mind screamed at her, declaring him a liar and a prevaricating fraud. Her heart was not so easily persuaded. Its cries were louder than the thoughts in her head. *Trust him,* it implored. *Read the evidence. He is worthy of your love!*

Still, confusion and turmoil filled her. By the time they returned to the Gardiner residence, her head ached, and she begged to be excused. Sally waylaid her on the way to her chamber.

"If you please, miss, this came for you." She extended the letter in her hand, and Elizabeth took it automatically. Instead of a thrill of anticipation, her heart sank. She was in no way ready to face Mr. Darcy—in written word or in person.

If only I had waited one more day to propose a meeting! She did not know how to proceed. Should she cry off? *I need to think.* Yes, contemplation would be just the thing. Elizabeth continued to her chamber. She tugged the drapes closed and lay down on the bed. The letter from Mr. Darcy she tucked into her pocket. Head pounding, she allowed her eyes to drift closed, welcoming the blissful relief of sleep.

When she awoke, it was still light out. Her head hurt less, and after a moment of disorientation, she recalled why she had taken to her bed in the middle of the day. No closer to an answer than before she went to sleep, Elizabeth sat up. The letter in her pocket rustled, and she pulled it out. Curiosity begged to be satisfied, but she instead tucked it into her writing case. *You will have to wait until I clear my head,* she told the letter. She could not have her reasoning clouded.

February 1812
Darcy House
Darcy

Darcy half-expected to find a letter from Elizabeth waiting for him the next morning. But, alas, the only missives in the post were from his aunt, Lady Catherine de Bourgh, imploring him to visit Rosings for St. Valentine's Day, and an invitation from Lady Matlock to dine next week.

Aunt Catherine's letter was very amusing. So humorous he found it that he went to the parlor, determined to share it with his sister. Still chuckling, he read it aloud.

Nephew,

I trust this letter finds you well, though I do not doubt that you have been busy, as usual, with matters of lesser importance than what truly deserves your attention. It is high time you remember your duty to your family and to the future of this estate, which, as you well know, must eventually be entrusted to my daughter's future husband. You will, no doubt, fulfil this obligation with honor and commitment.

I hereby inform you that you are expected at Rosings Park for St. Valentine's Day, which, as you must understand, is a most fitting occasion for reflection on matters of the heart, particularly those that concern the future of our family. I insist upon your presence at dinner on the evening of the fourteenth, where we shall discuss matters that are of utmost importance to us all. Your attendance is, of course, not optional. I trust you will find the time to pay your respects to your aunt, and to your betrothed, as is your duty.

As you may recall, since your infancy, it has been understood that Anne, my daughter, and you are to be united in marriage. This proposal, which has been discussed in every circle of our acquaintance for years, is not something to be taken lightly. I remind you that Anne's health, her composure, and her future happiness have always been linked to your regard, and it is now high time you acknowledge what has long been determined as the best course for your respective lines.

While you are at Rosings Park, I expect you to bring with you suitable tokens of your affection for your betrothed. It is no longer acceptable to treat this matter with the indifference I have observed on your part. I trust you will have the decency to present her with an appropriate gift that reflects your esteem. I shall leave the nature of this gift to your discretion, though I have no doubt that you will be capable of selecting something fitting for a lady of Anne's position and virtue.

As for your continued reluctance to fully commit to the arrangement, I must remind you that this is no trifling matter. It is a matter of family, of duty, and of ensuring that fortune and family line remain as they always have been. You owe it to your late father, to my dear departed sister, to me, and to Anne, to fulfill the obligations placed before you. No more excuses, no more delay. This union is inevitable, and I trust you will act with the seriousness and consideration it deserves.

I expect you here on the appointed day, and I will look forward to your bringing Anne the proper token that signifies your commitment to her, to our family, and to the preservation of the Darcy family's standing. Let us not forget the importance of this occasion.

Yours faithfully,
Lady Catherine de Bourgh

They laughed merrily at their aunt's presumption. This cradle engagement existed only in her mind—not even Lord Matlock thought the marriage would come about. Anne neared the age of five-and-twenty and would inherit Rosings Park in her own right at that time. Arrangements for his niece to take complete control of her estate had been made by Lord Matlock years ago. Aunt Catherine knew nothing of them, of course.

This was likely the reason she pressed him with more fervency than ever. Richard had often speculated as to their aunt's motives. "If she merely wished to preserve the family lines, why not have our cousin marry me?" It made sense. Richard was a second son and in need of a fortune. The truth was that Lady Catherine wished Anne to marry Darcy so he might whisk his bride away to the north, leaving *her* in control of Rosings Park.

"I am afraid I have another engagement on the fourteenth, Aunt," Darcy said, still chuckling as he tucked the letter into his pocket. Georgiana agreed and together they finalized the list of tokens Darcy needed to acquire before the appointed day.

His letter went unanswered the next day as well. And the next. By February 13th, Darcy was in full panic. Had something happened to Elizabeth? Had he erred in some way? What had occurred?

The answer came from an unlikely source. Bingley showed up the day before St. Valentine's Day, interrupting Darcy as he paced his study. All his business had been completed, and he was at sixes and sevens as his thoughts inevitably turned to Elizabeth.

"Darcy! You look dreadful. What is the matter? Are you ill?" Bingley strode in without being announced. He looked happier than Darcy ever recalled, and for a moment, he wished to banish his friend and his good cheer from the house.

Bingley sat in a chair next to the fire and put his feet on a stool. "Bad night?" he asked. "I know how you feel. Caroline is doing her utmost to ruin my engagement with Miss Bennet."

This caught his attention. "You proposed?" he asked.

"Yes. She accepted me, and we have her father's blessing. Darcy, I have never been happier in my life! To think I almost let her slip through my fingers."

"I am very pleased for you." In truth, he felt jealousy. *If only I could call Elizabeth mine,* he moaned. "Likewise, I am very sorry your sister is causing mayhem."

"Do you know what she did?" Bingley cried, pulling his feet off the stool and sitting up. "She followed me to Gunter's, where I planned to meet Jane and her relations. She imposed herself upon our gathering and then told the group—" he pitched his voice up to imitate Miss Bingley—"'How very...surprising...to see you all here. Together. Charles, when did you learn Miss Bennet was in town? Mr. Darcy tried to keep you too busy to discover her presence.' Rather, it was something of that nature."

Bingley chuckled humorously. "Goodness, I wanted to strangle her! Jane looked devastated. I do not plan to invite my sister to the wedding—in fact, I believe I shall follow through with my idea from the other day and not tell her until the deed is done."

Darcy was no longer listening. Miss Bingley's words repeated themselves over and over in his head. *This is the answer,* he thought. It had to be! He knew Elizabeth very well now—she would have seen it as a betrayal of trust learning that he had at first attempted to keep Bingley from her sister. *But that was so many months ago—before—*before the letters. Before he fully comprehended and acknowledged that he was completely and inextricably in love with her.

"If you will excuse me, Bingley, I have just remembered some business that cannot be delayed." He would write to her, beg for her understanding and forgiveness...

"Yes, of course." Bingley stood. "I have taken a lease on a town house down the row from you. That is what I came to say. I shall invite you to dinner next week." Without another word, Bingley left, whistling a merry tune as he went.

Darcy rushed to his desk and pulled a piece of paper towards him. There was no time to delay.

Dearest Elizabeth,

I find myself in the most disquieting state as I write these words to you. The past few days have been an unrelenting torture of uncertainty. I confess, after two days of silence from you, I feared the worst—some illness, or a family emergency, perhaps. Yet, my natural inclination to hold back from intrusion kept me silent. I reminded myself to be patient, knowing that whatever the cause, it was surely not for lack of affection on your part.

But then, as if fate itself were conspiring to break my heart, Mr. Bingley called upon me today. With his presence came an explanation I had not anticipated—an answer that, while clearing some fog, has only deepened the sorrow that has plagued me. It was then, hearing from him of Miss Caroline Bingley's actions, that I realized the great mistake I had made.

As I reflected on our last interaction and the painful silence that followed, I felt such regret, but none so poignant as for what I failed to see and share with you at the time. Miss Bingley's cruelty, which has so long tainted her words and actions, once again reared its ugly head. The incident in question—the one I thought had been resolved in the past—had I known its true weight, would have changed everything.

You see, I was convinced, erroneously, that your sister's affections were cold and that her reasons for not accepting Mr. Bingley were born more from your mother's urgings than from any true feeling on her part. It was this that caused me to follow him to town in November and prevail upon him to stay. He was persuaded to my way of thinking, which, unfortunately, united with that of Mrs. Hurst and Miss Bingley. He was miserable, but he believed our suppositions and did not return to Netherfield.

In my misguided attempt to shield Bingley from any further disappointment, I conspired with Miss Bingley to keep your sister's presence in town from him, certain it would only hurt him. I see now how wrong I was, and how much unnecessary harm that assumption has caused. Had I not attempted to read your sister's heart, or so fiercely believed in my own better judgment, I would have acted differently, and perhaps we would not now be facing this sorrow.

As I learned later, after receiving your letters, my error became so painfully clear. I immediately sought to remedy the situation and wrote to him, though I discovered, too late, that Bingley had already learned the truth and sought your sister out, clearing the way for their reconciliation. When Miss Bingley learned of this, her bitterness only grew. There seemed to be no need to bring the situation to your attention. And yet, my silence, I fear, may have prolonged your pain, and for that, I am most deeply sorry.

I did not tell you of the matter at the time, and that omission weighs heavily upon my conscience. I know that I cannot undo what has already been done, nor can I make up for the pain that my silence may have caused. However, I beg you to understand that my actions—though misguided—were born from a desire to protect and to preserve the happiness of those I care for most. Had I been more open, more candid, we may not have had the misunderstandings that have haunted us both.

If my failure to speak sooner has contributed to the return of the sentiments you felt last autumn, I ask you now to tell me plainly, and I will accept whatever consequences may come. But if, perhaps, you can find it in your heart to forgive me, I would ask for that chance, Elizabeth.

I must confess, my own happiness now depends on hearing your response. I shall wait for you tomorrow at the place we agreed, where I hope you will meet me, and if not, I will have my answer, and know at last whether all my efforts to atone for my missteps have been in vain.

With all the love I possess, and a heart full of hope,

Yours,
Fitzwilliam Darcy

He could do no more. Sanding and sealing the letter, he summoned a footman, giving him directions to see it delivered at once.

February 13, 1812
Gracechurch Street
Elizabeth

Elizabeth spent days deep in thought. Mr. Darcy's letter went unread, for she did not wish his sentiments to muddy her thoughts. Love is blind, or so she had heard, and she could not afford to make a mistake in this situation. Matters of the heart were complicated anyway, and marriage was a lifelong arrangement. If she intended to be Mrs. Darcy, she had best be certain she could fully trust the man before accepting any proposals. Yes, marriage. She had no doubt Mr. Darcy would ask, and she wished to have her answer ready when he did.

She considered what she knew of him. He was honorable, humble, and unafraid to admit when he was wrong. Through each letter, she had learned more of him, and fallen deeper in love with every word. Miss Bingley's pronouncement had cracked the illusion, and Elizabeth remembered every sin Mr. Darcy had committed since making his acquaintance.

But was she free of guilt? No, she had judged him harshly—*too harshly*. There had to be more to Miss Bingley's claims than she had presented. The lady was more than capable of putting words together in a way designed to cause offense, whilst also embellishing the truth.

On the morning of February 13th, Elizabeth felt she finally knew herself and understood what she wanted. She could not deny the love she felt for Mr. Darcy. He was human and therefore prone to error. How could she blame him for that? It was not as if his actions had any lasting damage. Jane was engaged to Mr. Bingley, and they were both very happy. And so she determined she would write to Mr. Darcy and tell him what she had learned. Then she would request his side of things—it was only fair to give him the chance to defend himself.

She opened his letter, eager to read that which she had set aside several days before. She had just read the greeting when Sally delivered another missive into her hands. A familiar thrill spread through her, warming her from head to toe. She read both and then began constructing a reply in her head.

Dearest Fitzwilliam,

Forgive the delay in my reply. Conflicting emotions warred within me, and I thought it best to wait before putting pen to paper. Your letters, as always, reach my heart in ways that words cannot fully express. It seems impossible that something as simple as ink and paper could stir me so deeply, and yet, when I read your thoughts, I feel as though you are right here with me, speaking those very words aloud. How can it be that I should find such delight in your written words, even when our separation feels most painful? You bring me peace in your letters, and though I long for the day we can speak face to face, I treasure the connection we share through these pages.

It is your words that truly comfort me. I read your letters again and again as I struggled with my emotions. The idea that we, together, have found a way to right the wrongs of the past gives me far greater joy than I know how to express. To be near you at last, to have the privilege of speaking with you in person, is all I can think of. Silence, even in the name of propriety, feels unbearable now that we have tasted the joy of these letters. If only we could share more than words! I find myself longing for the day when your thoughts and mine are no longer separated by distance, but are spoken directly to each other.

I find myself smiling in the quiet of my room at the mere recollection of your words! You bring such lightness into my life with your letters, and I confess to feeling that flutter in my chest when I open your missives, just as you describe. If you could know how your words leave a warmth in my heart that lingers long after they are read—how can it be that I feel more connected to you through ink than I do with anyone else in the world? It is a wonder, Fitzwilliam, a true wonder.

I cannot tell you how eagerly I anticipate our meeting on St. Valentine's Day. What a perfect moment it shall be! I am glad, too, that you seem willing to indulge me in speaking first, though I confess I fear my courage may falter in the face of your gaze. Your heart, I know, will be as full of emotions as mine. And though propriety calls for me to speak my thoughts, I suspect neither of us will be able to hold our feelings at bay for long. How could we, when they are so intertwined with our very hearts?

I shall be waiting for you by the fountain, and I know that whatever words we exchange, they will be ones that will forever change the course of our lives. I do not wish to speak only of the past—though it has shaped us and will continue to inform our future—but rather of what lies ahead. In you, Fitzwilliam, I have found a kindred spirit, and the thought of hearing your heart as you hear mine fills me with more hope and excitement than I could ever have imagined.

Until then, I remain, as always, yours most sincerely, and with a heart that is full to bursting.

Yours with affection,
Elizabeth

P.S. I shall wear my heart on my sleeve when I meet you, and I do hope you are prepared for the full force of my feelings. I have longed for this moment, and now that it is near, I feel as though all my hopes and dreams have led me to you.

She reread the letter. *Perfection,* she thought. He would be in no doubt of her wishes. Now she had only to wait until the morrow.

February 14, 1812
Hyde Park
Darcy

Darcy arrived at the designated spot an hour before the appointed time. He had spent the morning arranging the tokens of his love within a wicker basket. He had the usual things—a lovely card on which Georgiana had painted a watercolor—with a poem written on the back—a bouquet, and a small book of love poems wrapped in a silk cloth upon which his sister had painstakingly embroidered birds and flowers.

His little sister had been a great help. He was forced to admit that her impetuous decision to begin a correspondence with Elizabeth had turned out better than he could have hoped. All his objections about her family, her lack of wealth and connections, no longer mattered. He loved her, and that was enough to overcome every obstacle thrown in their path.

Her letter, which had arrived yesterday evening, was tucked into his pocket. His hand traveled there, touching the edge of the folded missive and recalling the hope and joy her words had brought him. Georgiana had noted his look of relief and remarked upon it. Sheepishly, he told her of Bingley's call and what he had learned. She approved of his haste in dispelling the remnants of mistrust that may have sprung up, and only complained a little when he refused to let her read Elizabeth's letter.

It was deeply touching and most definitely a love letter. Her words touched his very soul, and he longed to take her in his arms and kiss her passionately. *It is too bad we cannot do that in the park,* he grumbled. Still, he planned to offer himself to her that day, to beg her to be his wife. If—*when* she accepted, he would give her the final gift nestled in the basket. *Must think positively,* he told himself. He dared not imagine her refusing his offer of marriage. Darcy knew she would have no qualms about turning away an eligible match—she had refused her cousin, after all.

Despite her words of reassurance, his heart still beat erratically. Doubts threatened to consume him, and he paced in front of the fountain, checking his watch every few minutes. Time seemed to slow to a stop, and finally he collapsed on the edge of the fountain, putting his head in his hands and running his fingers through his carefully arranged hair.

The park was blessedly empty, and no one was around to witness his display. Taking a few deep breaths, he stood up and pulled on the hem of his jacket. The basket sat next to the fountain, its presence reminding him of the future that awaited, and filling him with courage.

"You are early." Elizabeth's teasing voice made him jump, and he turned.

Breaking into a grin, he stepped forward. "As are you, I see." Her hands were buried in a muff, and her cheeks were pink from the chill in the air. "Elizabeth." He came to a stop directly in front of her, reaching up to touch her cheek with a gloved hand.

"Good afternoon, Mr. Darcy." Elizabeth's eyes twinkled merrily, and he could see her feelings radiating out of them.

"I love you," he blurted out. "Most ardently." He swallowed painfully as emotion choked his throat. What would she say in reply?

Elizabeth's smile broadened and her gaze softened. "I love you, too, Fitzwilliam Darcy," she said. One hand came out of her muff, and she reached up to brush a lock of hair off his forehead. His hat wobbled precariously at her actions, and she steadied it before withdrawing her hand. "Never have I loved anyone as I love you," she continued. "We are so similar. Both are proud, defiant, and fiercely independent. We are stubborn to a fault, wilful, and headstrong." Her hand came to rest on his arm. "But also forgiving, compassionate, and understanding. Neither of us likes admitting when we are wrong, but we each have done our fair share of grovelling and asking for forgiveness. You are my match in every way."

"Then I have not lost you?" he murmured, stepping closer.

"Never."

Hang propriety, he thought. The park was empty anyway. He bent down and captured her lips with his own. It was everything he imagined and more. Her hand came to rest on his chest, and his arms went around her. After a few blissful moments, he broke away. "Marry me?" he asked breathlessly.

She beamed. "Yes."

Darcy let out an uncharacteristic whoop and swung her around in a circle. Elizabeth laughed delightedly as he did so, and her chuckles continued as he set her upon her feet. "Come with me," he said, taking her hand and leading her back to the fountain. "I have gifts for you!"

Her face fell. "I brought nothing for you!" she cried. "I did not even consider it."

Darcy pulled her into another embrace. "You have given me the best gift," he murmured huskily. "I have your love, and you will be my wife. Nothing can compare."

He pulled away and reached for the basket. Elizabeth exclaimed delightedly over each thing, particularly the last. He opened a dark blue velvet jewelry case and displayed a lovely necklace. There was something set behind the glass, similar to a mourning necklace, but more elaborate. The pendant was set in gold. Intricate flowers with emerald petals formed an oval around a glass center. Beneath the glass appeared to be a scrap of paper. He had written 'Love, Fitzwilliam' in his best script and had a jeweler set it.

"It is perfect!" she cried. Elizabeth lifted the pendant and admired it.

"There is an inscription on the back." Darcy took it and turned it over. She read it aloud.

"*For you, my heart—love unfeigned, bound by truth and unspoken devotion.*' Oh, Fitzwilliam!" She put it on, lightly touching the oval pendant and then taking his hand. "I shall treasure it always."

Heart full, he raised her hand to his lips and kissed it. "Forever and always, dearest Elizabeth."

Her tender expression grew curious. "Now that we are here and our future secured, I must know something—what prompted you to send the first letter?"

Darcy froze and then began to laugh. Tears rolled down his cheeks. "Oh, my love," he chortled. "Wait until I tell you..."

Epilogue

Worried as he was that she would be angry, Elizabeth thought the story of Georgiana beginning their correspondence to be rather humorous. Most of the letters had come from Mr. Darcy, but after being assured his sister had written as he would, she forgave them both and kissed him again. Intelligent lady that she was, Elizabeth reasoned it was Miss Darcy who had first written to Mr. Bingley and resolved to thank her for her interference as soon as possible.

When at long last they did meet, Georgiana Darcy greeted her future sister bashfully, only to receive an enthusiastic embrace and words of gratitude. She and Elizabeth became instant friends, sharing secrets and a sisterly bond almost as strong as the one between Elizabeth and Jane. Georgiana surprised her soon-to-be sister with a kitten. This caused her brother to groan and Elizabeth to exclaim in delight.

Darcy accompanied Elizabeth back to Gracechurch Street and was introduced to her aunt and uncle. He was pleasantly surprised at their genteel manner and thought they were both just the sort of people with whom he liked to associate. Mrs. Gardiner, shrewd and intelligent as her niece, demanded an explanation. Elizabeth's feelings were so different from the previous autumn that it made it difficult to believe she had fallen in love in so short a time. When everything was revealed, Mr. and Mrs. Gardiner, though scandalized at the flagrant disregard for propriety, thought the entire thing a good joke. Everything had ended well. Elizabeth and Mr. Darcy were engaged, so what harm was there in anything now?

The second express to Longbourn in less than a week was sent on its way before supper. Darcy felt eager to gain Mr. Bennet's consent. Elizabeth had included a note to her father explaining everything and asking for his blessing. She seemed a little nervous about it, explaining to her betrothed that she was her father's favorite daughter, and he might not be willing to part with her. To counter resistance, a second express was sent to Mrs. Bennet, informing her of the engagement. Any hopes Mr. Bennet had of quietly refusing the match were squashed, for Mrs. Bennet wasted no time in informing her neighbors that not one but two of her daughters were to be married to wealthy men.

Colonel Fitzwilliam had Mr. Wickham arrested and sent to debtor's prison before news of Darcy's engagement reached the ears of Elizabeth's neighbors. Gossip whirled about his arrest, and soon tales of his wrong-doings spread throughout Meryton. Everyone was pleased to paint the officer as a villain, especially when news of Elizabeth's good fortune was widely known. It spoke well of Mr. Darcy that he would marry a local lady. The gossip grew until others insisted Elizabeth had hidden her courtship with Mr. Darcy to protect their privacy. Why else would she refuse Mr. Collins, who by all accounts was a worthy suitor as well?

Mrs. Bennet threw herself into planning a lavish wedding. Both couples insisted on waiting no more than a month, and so she flew into a frenzy, arranging everything properly. The ladies stayed in town until their wedding clothes were purchased. This served two purposes: they remained close to their respective betrothed, and could continue courting away from Mrs. Bennet's prying eyes and inappropriate comments.

Jane and Elizabeth Bennet married their respective gentlemen on a Friday in the second week of March. Resplendent in their wedding finery, their father led them down the aisle. Mary and Kitty stood up with their sisters, much to the annoyance of the youngest, Lydia. Already petulant because she would not be the first to marry, she scowled during the entire ceremony. Everyone cheerfully ignored her.

Miss Bingley and the Hursts did not attend. Bingley kept his word and did not inform them of the event until after it happened. Caroline, still believing she would be able to separate her brother from the unsuitable country miss, flew into a rage. Her resulting tantrum caused enough damage to the Hurst townhouse that Mr. Hurst demanded she be cast out. With nowhere else to go, she went north to stay with an aunt in Yorkshire.

As the carriages trundled away from the wedding breakfast, the fading echoes of celebration seemed to retreat into the distance, leaving behind a serene silence that enveloped Elizabeth and Darcy. The rhythmic clatter of the horses' hooves was the only sound that marked the passing of time, and for a moment, it felt as though the entire world had faded away, leaving only the two of them to bask in the quiet joy of their union.

Elizabeth, her heart full, allowed her head to rest gently against Darcy's shoulder, the comfort of his presence bringing a sense of completeness she had never before known. His steady warmth beside her, his strength in the simplest of gestures, filled her with a profound peace. She had long wondered if such a love—genuine, unpretentious, and deep—was ever truly possible, and now she knew it was. She had found it. *They* had found it.

"Love unfeigned," she whispered, her voice low but certain, as though the words were not just a reflection of her own heart but of the truth she now saw so clearly. "There is no other treasure so valuable in the world."

Darcy turned his gaze upon her, the weight of her words settling in his heart. His love for her was as vast as it was tender, and yet, it had not always come easily. She knew he had struggled at times to trust in the possibility of happiness, to believe that someone steadfast and genuine could ever truly be his. But in her presence, he had found a peace he had never thought attainable—a peace that had nothing to do with the expectations of society or the constraints of propriety, and everything to do with the simplicity of loving and being loved in return.

He pressed a kiss to her hair, his lips brushing the soft strands. She savored the quiet intimacy of the moment. "Yes," he murmured, his voice thick with emotion. "And we are most fortunate to be in possession of so rare a gift." He paused, his hand gently resting against hers, feeling the weight of what they had just promised each other. The vows they had spoken that morning were not just words—they were the foundation upon which they would build their lives, a testament to the love that had blossomed between them, steadfast and unshakable.

As they sat in the quiet of the carriage, a shared understanding passed between them. Neither spoke of it, but both knew that this love, this rare and precious treasure, would be tested. Life would bring its challenges, as it always did, but they now faced the future together. They would navigate the unknown with courage, side by side. There would be days of uncertainty and nights of doubt, yet they had vowed, in that moment, to meet whatever came with the same unwavering devotion they had promised each other at the altar.

The future stretched out before them, full of promise, but not without its share of unknowns. Elizabeth's thoughts turned to the years ahead—the home they would make together, the family they might one day raise, the quiet moments of joy and the times of hardship that would shape their lives. She thought of their shared adventures, of traveling, of growing together, and of finding new ways to cherish each other every day. She knew, with a certainty that filled her heart, that no matter what life might bring, their love would be their constant.

Darcy, too, thought of the future. He spoke softly in her ear of the promise he had made to her—to always seek her happiness above all else. He vowed to protect her, honor her, and cherish her as no one ever had. "I will strive, day by day, to be the husband you deserve, to be a man worthy of the love you have so generously given me." In the quiet strength of her presence, he found a steadiness he had never known before. The weight of his past mistakes, the misunderstandings, the pride, the prejudice—all of it had led him to this moment, and he would do all in his power to ensure that their days together would be filled with peace, with laughter, and with the same unfeigned love they had discovered so unexpectedly in each other.

The future did indeed hold uncertainties, but in that moment, they both knew that together, they could conquer the world. Their vows would guide them, and the love they shared would be their foundation, their anchor, and their light.

As the carriage rolled on its journey, they sat in companionable silence, each savoring the quiet joy of the day, their hearts light with the knowledge that they were, at last, home in each other. And as the world outside moved on, Elizabeth and Darcy silently vowed that they would do everything within their power to deserve this rare and precious treasure—the love unfeigned that they had found in one another.

Other Books by MJ Stratton

Other Books by MJ Stratton
Note: Books with an asterisk are redemption stories
Darcy and Lizzy Variations:
A Far Better Prospect**
When Given Good Principles**
No Less Than Any Other
The Lake House at Ramsgate
Thwarted
To Marry for Love
Other Stories:
The Redemption of Lydia Wickham**
Catherine Called Kitty**
Mary, Marry? Quite Contrary!**
Charmed
Charming Caroline**
From Another Perspective
Crossroads
Variations from Jane Austen's other works
What Ought to Have Been**

Thank you for reading!

Acknowledgements

Acknowledgements

A special thank you to everyone (betas, editors, ARC participants) who helped me along with this book. A special thanks to Rebecca, Gratia, and Shannon for your efforts to help make this book free of error.

And, as always, thank you to my darling husband, who has supported me through it all, especially when it came to finding time to write while still being a wife and mom. From the inception of this story to completion has been a rollercoaster at our house! Thank you for your support!

About The Author

About The Author

MJ Stratton is a long-time lover of Jane Austen and her works, whose much-beloved aunt introduced her to Pride and Prejudice at the age of sixteen. The subsequent discovery of Austenesque fiction sealed her fate. After beta reading and editing for others for nearly a decade, MJ started publishing her own work in 2022. MJ balances being a wife and mother with writing, gardening, sewing, and many other favorite pastimes. She lives with her husband and four children in the small, rural town where she grew up.

Printed in Great Britain
by Amazon